☼

dead bunnies

by

k.j. stevens

crooked steeple press
7868 smith road
alpena, michigan 49707

Books by k.j. stevens

A Better Place
A Place to Land
A Prayer
Infidelity
Dead Bunnies
Landscaping

The author would like to send special thanks to the editors and staff at the following publications for taking time to read and publish his writing:

The Adirondack Review
Fluid Magazine
Me Three
Circle Magazine
Cellar Door
Prose Ax
WriteGallery
David Coyote's Den
East of the Web
BloodLotus
Temenos

☼

~ For Brandi ~

☼

dead bunnies

Contents

introduction

This is Dead Bunnies. A collection of stories. Old and new. Some previously published. Some unknown. All of them together. Here. Now. For you. Because time is running out. These days will not last. Shiny things fade. And all we are left with are stories. Our memories made and moments lost.

In conversation. Letters. Pictures. And in song.

We must speak. Be heard. And share.

This book is dedicated to my family and friends. Without you, it would only be me. Sitting in the old house. Next to the old church. Near the cemetery. Typing away. Shoving stories into boxes and desk drawers. But you've been here. Always. With me from the beginning. And you've held on. Through snow drifts, muddy trails, and winding curves. The ride has often been rough, but we've always made it safe and sound.

So far.

Always breaking through.

To the good stuff.

On the other side.

This book is dedicated to Brandi. A beautiful young woman, an aspiring writer, an honest soul. Fourteen stories. One for each year she walked this earth. I wish we would have had more time. But as we know all too well, good things do not last and more often than not we are left empty-handed. Standing alone. Struggling to fill heart and mind. With sense. Feeling. Memory. A little something to get us through. To keep us going. So that we can fight the good fight. And keep on keepin' on.

your faithful correspondent,

~ K.J.

the throw away

✿
skipping church

My feet were braced against the dashboard. My fingers gripped the edge of the seat. The truck skidded to a stop in the church parking lot. When the dust settled, I could see that Dad was halfway through his peppermint schnapps. One hand draped over the steering wheel. The other in his lap, clutching the pint. Dad's face and neck were sweaty. The collar and underarms of his blue t-shirt were wet. He took another pull from his bottle.

"Here we are, Church girl! Go get what you need!"

I opened the door and jumped out. Most of the congregation had already filed into the church. Father Touchstone was at the door, greeting the stragglers.

"Making it to church today, Abby?"

I held the dress down against my legs and walked up the steps.

"No sir, Dad's not feeling well today."

He smiled sympathetically then looked past me. Dad was honking the horn, yelling at people as they passed.

"Has your Dad been drinking again?"

My face grew hot. My tongue tied up. I slipped by him and made my way to the greeting table. As usual, Father Touchstone had laid an offering. Three boxes of plain donuts and a pot of coffee. It was an idea that Mom had proposed to him a year earlier. It would help bring people together, she told him. And when people came together, especially in The House Of The Lord, it created a shared energy, and eventually this sharing would bring to light the real discovery of God.

11

It was something that all of us needed, Mom said. To find the light of God and to feel His energy. And it came to everyone she said, at some point and time, no matter who they were. The Lord's ways weren't all that mysterious. The mystery was that more and more people were having a harder time finding Him and His Truth.

At times, it took something very special, she said. Like marrying your soul mate, or the birth of a child. Other times it was simple. Like a walk along the shore of Lake Huron during a brilliant sunrise. Or apple blossoms in full bloom. But for those that were stubborn, for those whose last hope was to be saved or retreat into the arms of the Devil, it took something more. A stray bullet during hunting season and the loss of a limb. A capsized boat and passengers that cannot swim. A silent night ripped to pieces as a car accident throws the blanket of coma. When a person was touched, it would be clear, she said. The soul would be awakened. Perceptions altered. And one would gain insight beyond her years.

I didn't know if I wanted to be awakened. Didn't know if I needed it. In fact, God was far from my mind as I stood there before the donuts and steaming coffee, staring at the church's community bulletin board.

As usual, it was plastered with garage sales, intramural sport schedules, and items lost and found. The PETS LOST list was long. By the curve and slant of the handwriting, I could tell Touchstone had written it. Probably taking notes from phone calls and discussions throughout the week then copying the list over to a clean sheet of white poster board. Saturday night so that on Sunday it could be seen by the congregation. The list was alphabetized and some of the names were accompanied by small pictures.

SPRING HAS SPRUNG, it read. *AND PETS LIKE TO RUN. IF YOU HAVE ANY KNOWLEDGE AS TO THE WHEREABOUTS OF THESE FAMILY FRIENDS PLEASE CONTACT ME @ 989-354-8248.*

The list began with Art, a six-year-old black-and-white Tabby wearing a blue collar. He was last seen crossing the railroad tracks on LaComb Road. It ended with Zeus, a two-year-old Black Lab. Last seen chasing a cottontail near Male's Corner.

When I heard Dad revving the engine, I decided I'd better hurry. I looked away from the PETS LOST list to the cover of the most recent Sunday program. On it, a daisy was drooping over to shield a butterfly from a downpour of rain. I thought the picture was nice. That the flower and the butterfly were especially bright against the darkness of rain, but I doubted the picture's truth because I'd never seen a butterfly caught in the rain.

Dad blasted the horn. I took two of the Sunday programs and two of the donuts then ran out the door past Touchstone.

"Abby!" he called. "Is your mother working again, today?"

I turned to him as I reached the truck. His skin, already tan from a spring generous with sunlight, was dark against his white collar. The sun was bright on his face and as he squinted into the light, his mouth eased into a dimpled smile. I squeezed the programs in my hand and thought of how happy Mom would be to hear that he had asked about her.

"Yes, she's working again," I said.

"It's a shame she has to work sundays," he said, as he looked past me and glared at Dad. "But make sure you tell her that I liked her suggestions for next week's program. Her creativity is a blessing."

Dad leaned across the seat and stuck his head out the passenger window.

"Why don't you mind your own business, you nosey sonofabitch!"

"Well, good morning to *you*, Mr. Kolozkowski! Good to see you're up and about this morning!"

"Aw, go to hell!"

I ran to the truck, opened the door and leapt inside. The donuts and Sunday programs dropped from my hand onto the ground. I slammed the door and sank out of sight. Hugged my knees and doubted ever returning to church as Dad spun us out of the driveway, onto the road, and maneuvered the familiar rights and lefts that led us to the county dumping grounds.

✿
the smell

I knew where we were at all times by the bumps and turns. By the shudder and shifting of the truck. The first stretch of road, Cathro Road, was paved and hilly. My insides lifted and rolled as we passed over the hill crests. I looked out the window. Saw cows grazing, standing, laying. All of them at the bottom of a steep grade near a pool of brown water.

People lost their cows down there, Dad had told me once. Because cows liked to wander. Into the woods, past the pool, they'd mosey along looking for something to chew, and suddenly they'd find their wide, heavy bodies being sucked into the mud. Thick black muck that Dad said reeked like rotting potatoes. A smell I had not known until the day I was trying on clothes at the dumps.

There'd been shirts, dresses, pants, and shoes piled up between an overturned refrigerator and a gutted-out sofa. I'd found a mirror nearby and propped it up against the sofa, so that I had my own makeshift fitting room. I tried on whatever looked new or clean. Marched back and forth in front of the broken mirror, and was amazed as my reflection changed shape and size in the glass, and I could see glimpses of what I'd look like one day.

The rotting smell came to me as I sat on the side of the refrigerator and tried on a pair of sandals. It was a strange smell, different from the normal sweets and sours of spoiled food, dead animals, and mildewed papers, so it only took a moment for me to follow my nose to the source. To the refrigerator I was sitting on.

I stood. Paused for a minute with my fingers around the door handle, and I thought of the nightly news reports. Children locking themselves in discarded refrigerators during games of hide-and-seek. Parents sobbing on tv, warning the world to get rid of any old appliances that might be lurking in the yard, basement, or garage. Through fits of tears, choking on his words, a father telling other fathers to at least chain and padlock the doors of these silent killers.

I imagined opening the refrigerator to a dead little girl, like me. Her face swollen and purple. Her mouth stretched into a howl for help. Tears stained into her cheeks. Her hands silent at her side, black and blue from pounding on the door.

"Abby! Where are you?" Dad yelled.

He had been standing on a toilet. Scanning the dumping grounds for me.

"Over here!" I yelled.

He waved. I waved back. Then I covered my nose and mouth and opened the door.

I was disappointed. The refrigerator was white and clean and empty. Nothing purple or swollen. No silenced scream.

I bent down and put my head inside. The smell crept around my fingers. Burned my nostrils. And my stomach lurched. I moved to open the vegetable drawer at the bottom of the refrigerator and I remembered hearing stories about babies stuffed in garbage cans and boxes, plastic bags and backpacks. And I believed I might find a baby of my own. Crammed into the drawer by some strung-out mother, or crack-addict Dad. Another baby left for dead.

And then there would be cops and reporters, all sorts of nosey types stomping through the dumps. In hip boots and gas masks. Investigating. Invading our space. Wondering what it was that Dad and I were doing at the dumps anyway. It would be national news. Scandalous. And I could see Mom in the livingroom. Rocking in her chair. Hand over her heart. Hyperventilating. But when I opened the drawer, the mess was simple. A black pool of liquid oozing from an open bag of rotting potatoes. Smelling worse than dead skunks, maggoty meat, or a hot pile of dirty diapers. And I felt bad for the cows as we passed and left them behind because I knew that somewhere one of them was wandering and it would sink, suffocate, and slowly die in that awful smell.

✿
the good book

Dad veered us off Cathro Road. Wheeled us into the parking lot. He hopped out and picked up a cracked flower pot.

"That goddamned Touchstone. Why in the hell is he so nosey? What's it to him if your Mom don't make it to church? He's not God. If God were alive I bet he'd be right here with me in the trash. Even God would like dump pickin'."

Dad tossed the flower pot to the ground. Kicked through a pile of moldy magazines. At the bottom of the pile he found a book. He opened it and fanned through the pages. They were white and clean.

"Jesus Christ! Looky here! A copy of *Where The Red Fern Grows!* You ever read this?"

"I've never heard of it," I said.

"See, if you spent more time with your old man, you'd already have read this book."

He closed it and handed it to me.

"There, this is for you. I think you'll like it. If we find a pen that works I'll sign it and write a little note in it for you."

"A note? For what?"

"Cause that's what you're supposed to do when you give someone a book. You're supposed to write a little note in it and sign your name. Like when you memorized all those prayers and verses and Touchstone gave you that Bible."

Dad was looking all around on the ground for a pen.

"You can sign it when we get home, Dad."

"Yeah, I guess it can wait. What the hell did he write in the old good book, anyway?"

"He wrote, '*May you read this with God in your heart,*'" I answered.

"Yeah! That's it! '*God in your heart!*' Like you need a book, or some holy-roller telling how to get God."

Dad moved along ahead of me. I tucked the book under my arm and followed.

✿
dump pickers

We weren't the only ones at the dumps. There was an old man. Carrying a green bucket. Following his even older looking wife. They moved slowly, but deliberately through the trash. The old man kept a perfect, measured distance from the old woman so that when she stopped, fell to her knees and examined something more closely, he could stand behind her, bucket at arms length, waiting.

But his focus was drawn elsewhere. To a young woman wearing a tight, tie-dyed shirt, blue jean shorts, and yellow hip boots. She was carrying a large, red mesh onion sack over her shoulder and wearing a sun hat. She moved over the ground slowly, stopping every other step or so to lift something out of the garbage with her yellow, rubber-gloved hands and put it in the sack. She was a regular. And she was pretty. I'd seen her close up once before. On a Sunday morning, as Dad and I searched through appliances looking for a new toaster. She was wearing the same boots and the same gloves, but instead of a tie-dyed shirt, she was wearing a tight, yellow half-shirt. She had approached us, she said, because she was interested in a lampshade that I'd been carrying around for most of the morning.

"It's not for sale," Dad said, as he looked her over, his gaze pausing at her tan midriff.

"But it matches a lamp that I have," she said.

"Tough shit, missy."

She persisted.

"I'll give you five bucks for it."

20

Dad looked at me. Rolled his eyes.

"Listen, missy. This is just a suggestion, but maybe instead of poking around in the household furnishings, looking for a top for your lamp, you might want to consider visiting the clothing section and finding one for yourself."

She looked at me. Smiled. Shook her head and walked away. She wasn't angry or disappointed. Maybe she didn't even really want the lampshade anyway. Sometimes, when you're at the dumps, all you really want is someone to talk to.

Since Dad was already busy searching, I walked over to the old man. He was still staring at the young woman, watching her long, careful strides.

"Finding anything good today?" I asked.

He broke his gaze from her and shook his head as if I'd startled him from a dream. He tilted the bucket toward me. It was filled with light-blue saucers and cups. And they matched. Which was a rarity.

"We found these just over there beyond the canoe," he said. "There are more of them if you want some. We only needed a set of four."

"Joshua!" His wife piped up. "You're not supposed to give things away. People need to find them on their own."

The old man rolled his eyes at her then smiled at me. He reached into his pocket, fished around for a moment, then held out a fist. He asked me to close my eyes and open my hand.

"No peeking," he said. "And if you can guess what it is, I'll let you have it."

I felt its surface. It was smooth and warm and oval-shaped.

"Abby!" Dad yelled from behind me.

I opened my eyes. Turned. And looked over at him. He was holding up an iron.

"Does Mom need one of these?"

"I don't know!" I shouted back.

The old woman was on her knees. Scraping away at something. Giggling. I couldn't tell if it was at me, at Dad, or at what she had found.

When I turned back to the old man, he was looking at my hand.

"It's an egg," he said.

It was small and blue. Like a robin's egg. But it was heavy and solid all the same.

"Ceramic," he said. "So it'll last."

He turned to watch the tie-dyed woman again. But she was far away, nearly out of his sight, walking to the parking lot. I thanked the old man, put the egg in my pocket, and walked toward Dad.

He was holding the iron up high. By the cord. Like a fisherman with his trophy.

"Pretty nice, ain't it?"

He dangled it in front of my face.

Dad knew finding things for Mom, things she could use, was a way to soften her. Mom would eventually discover that we had missed services again and this coupled with Dad's drinking was forgivable only by presenting her with gifts.

"What do you think?" he asked.

It was a little tarnished, but the cord was in tact and there weren't any buttons missing.

"I think she'll like it," I said.

He shook it back and forth.

"It's still got water in it!" he said. "Must be a recent drop off!"

He gave it to me, then knelt down to rummage through a box of old newspapers. I held the iron and I thought of Mom, and I wondered if she ever smelled the dumps in our clothes when she did the laundry on Sunday nights. Scrubbing and rinsing. Scrubbing and rinsing. Trying to wash away the dumps. Dad's drinking. And the wandering nature of her little girl. So that we could be a normal family. A studious, God-fearing daughter, who went to church and said her prayers. A stay-at-home mom who baked cookies and raised a garden of roses and daffodils instead of beets and potatoes. And a sober father who worked a steady job. Spending his nights and weekends at home. Mowing the lawn. Washing the car. Taking out the trash instead of bringing it home.

☼
bears

I knew that Dad would be busy with the papers awhile, so I set *Where the Red Fern Grows* down next to him and put the iron on top of it. I walked away. Over broken bottles, crumpled papers, and dead aerosol cans. Toward the sinkhole. And I remembered the only time that Mom had made it to the dumps. When Dad parked the truck and we sat in the dark. Waiting for the bears.

She'd been happy that day. Because all of us had made it to church. Because Dad had waited till after noon to start drinking. And because we were just another family. Together. In our Sunday best. Taking a drive. Her smile never faded. She remained cheerful and warm. Even as Dad cracked a fresh pint and drove us to the dumping grounds.

There were a half-dozen other cars parked around the dumps. Men and women. Boys and girls. Packed into old pickup trucks, station wagons, and sedans. All of us sitting and waiting. Watching the red-orange sun dissolve behind the horizon. Watching stars come to life. One by one. Tiny white specks in the darkening sky.

Mom sighed.

"Little doorways to Heaven. That's what those are."

Dad swigged at his bottle.

"Don't be gettin' all religious on us," he said. "They're just lights in the sky."

He opened his window to spit. The crickets were singing.

"Turn off the engine so we can hear them better," Mom said.

"No. We're not here for crickets. We're here for bears."

24

He rolled up the window.

"We keep windows closed and engines running."

I looked up through the cracked windshield at the stars.

"They look like eyes," I said.

Dad took another drink, then looked up at the sky.

"Eyes, hey?"

"They *do* look like eyes," Mom said.

Dad capped his bottle. Set it under his seat.

"Okay, smarties. If they *are* eyes, which way are they looking? In, or out?"

"Out," I said.

"Out," Mom whispered. "At the light."

Then came the headlights. One set after another. Including ours. Pushing away stars. Flooding the night. Showing us the bears. Shiny-eyed and black. Pawing through garbage. Huddled near the part of the sinkhole where Dad always told me not to go. Three big ones and three little ones. Very aware of the headlights. Of us. But unafraid. Sticking close together. Near the edge. Where it wasn't quite light and it wasn't quite dark, and they looked like shadows within the shadows.

"It's beautiful," Mom whispered.

"Beautiful," I said.

We were warm and cozy in the truck. In the amber glow of the dashboard lights. Lullabied by cricket song. My eyes grew tired. My body grew light. Dad reached to hold Mom's hand. And I fell away. Gently. Into the space between them.

✿
sinkhole

When I reached the edge of the sinkhole, I looked back toward Dad. He looked like any other man reading the Sunday paper, except that he wasn't in the livingroom lounging in his favorite chair. He was sitting on a blown-out tire, reading a paper that had turned black in places.

Going near the sinkhole was like a cow wandering into the mud. That's what Dad had once told me. That when people wandered too near the edge, they disappeared. Some were dragged off by bears, but most were sucked away into the sinkhole, immobilized and choked to death by everything broken and rotting.

I stepped closer to the hole and the warnings ran through my head. The edge like quicksand. People falling in. And I imagined being buried alive by garbage. Trying to scream for help. Taking in mouthfuls of hair, cigarette butts, and dirty Band-Aids. Darkness closing in and my head poking out of the trash just enough so that I could see the bears roaming in.

But, like other childhood warnings, these only sparked curiosity and pushed me closer to the edge.

The air was thick and foul and it was difficult to breathe. I thought about dead cows and rotting potatoes, and I measured my movements carefully. When I felt sure-footed enough, I knelt down and looked over the edge.

It was then that I could see the smell. Beyond broken chairs, stained mattresses, and rusty box springs, I could see all of it. Dead deer and dead opossums mostly, but also cats and dogs. Rib cages and skulls.

Matted fur and stiff bodies. Legs outstretched, forever frozen in a run. And suddenly, I thought of something terrible.

Moms and Dads finding dead pets. Dogs mangled in the middle of the street. Cats flattened near the driveway. Parents working quickly. Wrapping cold bodies in old blankets. Stuffing them into garbage bags. Putting them in car trunks, truck beds, or behind seats. For a ride to the dumps. To throw part of their family there. Just over the edge of the long, sloping hill. Dumping dead pets into the sinkhole. Hoping that eventually everything would be sucked away.

I imagined kids coming home from school, asking where their pets had gone. And parents answering as they always did, that Scruffy or Daisy had run away, but that it was okay because sooner or later they'd turn up. All an animal wanted was just some space to run, they'd say.

I remembered seeing missing cats and dogs on the church bulletin board, and some of them were the animals heaped before me. But now they were without eyes. Missing fur. Had broken legs. And dead, flat tails. None of them would ever run. And none of them would ever return home. No matter how many posters were put up and not matter how many prayers were said.

Dad shouted for me.

"Abby! Where the hell are you?"

I turned to call to him and at once I began to slide. Down the slope of the sinkhole. On my belly. Things wet and hard, soft and metallic, brushed and scraped my body. I felt my dress tearing and rough unknown edges cutting my skin. I held my head up. Tried to scream, but the smell filled me.

When I opened my eyes I was staring into the sky. Seagulls were sailing. Their wings outstretched. Calling. I sat up and checked myself over for anything broken. My body was covered in brownish-black muck and everything was sticking to me. Q-tips, disposable razors, and gobs of animal hair. My skin was stinging.

"Abby!"

I looked up. Dad was on his belly, leaning over the edge. I tried to stand, but felt my body sinking. My hands, knees and feet pushed through the muck.

"Help me, Daddy!"

"Don't stand up, honey! Just crawl as close to me as you can!"

The old man appeared and kneeled at Dad's side. His face was white with fear. I knew that in all of it I had probably lost his egg.

"I've got a rope in my truck!" The old man shouted, "Hold on!"

He got up and I could hear him running away.

"We'll get you out of there! Don't worry! Just hold on!" Dad called.

I crawled as far as I could, then waited. I looked at where I'd been and the spot where I'd fallen was filling in with debris. Further down the slope flies were buzzing all around a hound. Its belly was huge. One of its legs was missing. I tried not to look at it, but I felt it was looking at me.

I imagined being sucked down under the dead animals into the greasy soil and entering a dark hole where things touched you, breathed on you, and fed on you. I would be underground with cows and lost dump pickers. All of us part of that rotting potato smell. Dad would be asking, "Where's God now? Where's this God that would pull a girl into a

28

sinkhole?" Mom would hide away, cooking, scrubbing, seeking guidance from the Bible. Touchstone would offer his condolences. And in the end, my life would be a sad, unfortunate tragedy. Everyone would know about me. Abby, the girl who skipped church to pick through people's throwaways. My life would be a warning to children everywhere, like the martyrs of the refrigerator world.

"Are you hurt?" Dad asked.

My skin burned.

"I don't know," I said.

"Just hold tight!"

Dad got up, and I could hear him running away.

The dead hound's eyes stared at me. I took a deep breath to try to calm the sobs that I felt coming and it was then that I noticed I couldn't smell. That none of what surrounded me was coming through. I took another deep breath. Still, I could not smell. The hound continued his dead stare so I leaned back into the garbage away from his gaze. Suddenly, I remembered that I had read *Where the Red Fern Grows*. I had read it in school for a book report. It was about a boy and his hound. Or two hounds...two hounds and hunting. Or was it something else? And what did that book mean to me? I thought for sure that this was something that Touchstone and Dad would have in common. That most men, when boys, had read that book and that they had liked it. That they had maybe even cried when they read it and they hadn't told anyone but God because there was no getting around that whether you believed in Him or not. And, I thought, maybe the old man had read it too. And that reading it had made a difference. That it had it maintained some softness inside of him during his movements through a hard world. And because he had read it, he had been there that day to give me the egg. I reached into my pocket for it and it was gone.

I sat up and felt my body sink again, so I laid back down and thought of the old man running to get the rope. His old heart hammering away. His feet pounding through garbage. Would he make it to the rope? And why was he running? A little girl over the edge. Into a hole where the bears roam. What did it matter? Children died every day. In refrigerators at home. Or in places like the dumps.

All of it turned and twisted inside of me and I thought of how good it could be if I could just stay there, where I was. My shoes sucked away by the muck. My Sunday dress torn and hanging off me. And then I heard the commotion. The old man, the old woman, and Dad. Up there above me. Calling my name.

Grab onto the rope, Abby! they yelled. *Grab on and don't let* go!

And in my new place at the bottom of the pit, everything that should have felt suffocating and cold, felt good. I felt like I was sleeping. That all of what I had known had been a dream. And that my being there in the sinkhole, covered in garbage was real and true, and that it might be a good picture for the cover of a Sunday program because it was as believable as a butterfly caught in the rain.

grasshoppers

☼

Outside under the late summer sun, searching for wild strawberries, picking and eating them as I find them. My fingers sticky and stained red. Bees and flies buzzing me. Sunshine burning my skin. My feet sore and itchy from being barefoot in the field. Growing tired and bored, so I walk through our long backyard to the house.

Dad's at the kitchen table. Clenching a white pen. Scribbling numbers into his checkbook.

"Dad, can we go fishing?"

"Not now."

"But there's nothing to *do*."

A deep crease wedges between his bushy eyebrows. This is a STOP sign. *Do not push things. Give me time*, it says. He scratches more figures.

Envelopes, stamps, and papers clutter the table. I reach to help.

"I can stamp envelopes for you."

"Not with those sticky paws."

Dad takes my hands. Turns them over. Smells the strawberry scent and takes a deep breath. A smile eases in. Rises.

"Okay. We'll go fishing. But first, I need to pay these bills."

I lean on the table, content to wait.

"What are you doing?" he asks.

"Waiting."

"No, not here. The best thing you can do is find bait. Then when I'm done we'll just have to grab our gear and go."

"I'll dig worms," I say, turning to go.

"No. We need grasshoppers."

"Grasshoppers? Why?"

"How do you suppose I caught all those bass when I was a kid?"

"Didn't you use worms?"

"I used worms for little fish. I caught big ones with grasshoppers."

In an instant, I'm ransacking the cupboard under the kitchen sink, searching for an empty cottage cheese carton. I find one and head for the door. Dad rises from the table.

"No. No. No. You can't use that."

At the pantry, he takes a coffee jar from a shelf. Unscrews the cap. Shakes dusty coffee remains into the sink. He rinses the jar. The white sunlight through the kitchen window is bright on his big hands. Water runs over them like liquid diamonds.

He dries the jar and gives it to me.

"Why a jar?"

"It's what I used when I was a kid."

I turn to go. Dad calls after me.

"When you get out there, stay away from the Oxford place!"

"What if there are grasshoppers in their yard?"

"Then we'll dig worms."

Dad returns to bills.

I walk outside.

✿

The sunny-hot steps roast my feet. I shift from foot to foot, toe to heel, looking over the front yard for a place to start. A grasshopper flies up from the lawn and buzzes into a patch of daisies near the road. I walk toward it, scouting the ground for movement and I spook three white cabbage moths into the air. They weave and loop like they're playing drunken follow-the-leader.

And this is when I hear a car.

THE CAR.

Knocking engine. Whistling radiator. Whirring snow tires on hot summer pavement. Mr. Oxford and his big, old Lincoln Continental roaring home.

Mr. Oxford is a bony, sick looking man on medical leave from his duties as a music professor at Oak Grove Community College. He is a drunk, and he and his wife own the only other house on our short, dead end road. A small, powder-blue home with yellow shutters. They have a large front yard that's stuck full of painted posts. Yellow posts holding bird houses. White posts supporting bird feeders. Mrs. Oxford appears once in the morning and once at night to check the feeders and fill them if they need it. I wave to her when I see her, but she never waves back.

Mr. Oxford must be really lubed up because he's got the Lincoln growling like a mean machine, swerving all over the road.

The cabbage moths bounce along above the asphalt. They circle round and round as the Lincoln barrels toward them. They make a tall, narrow loop, then fall lazily into the car's path. Two of them are gobbled up into the grill. Sucked under the hood before I can even bat an eyelid.

The lucky one, the lone survivor, is pushed under the car then rocketed up out the back-end like a scrap of paper. It hovers flatly for a moment then flutters to the road. It sits folding and unfolding its wings, testing for flight, then rises up and drifts over a field of purple clover. I watch it in the bright sky until my eyes hurt.

Mr. Oxford slams his car door.

He staggers out of the Lincoln. White hair standing in frizzy tufts. Legs skinny and pale in black, baggy shorts. He's carrying a box of wine in one arm and a case of Stroh's under the other. He lumbers toward the house, yelling.

"If that door is locked, woman, I'm gonna brain you!"

At the door, all loaded up, he struggles to get in.

"For crissakes! Why'd you lock the damned door?"

Mrs. Oxford opens the door. She is tall and thick, has bushy red hair. She is a giant of a woman and every time I see her I'm amazed that Mr. Oxford has the courage, or stupidity, to treat her like he does.

Mr. Oxford shoves the box of wine into her hands and pushes past her. She is left standing in the doorway, looking outside. Her big hands cover the wine box entirely. I wave to her but she must not see me because she turns and closes the door.

Once they're inside, I turn wholeheartedly to the task at hand. Catching grasshoppers. Chasing and kneeling. Chasing and kneeling. But the grasshoppers are getting the best of me. Scrapes from picker-bushes. Skinned knees. Sunburned arms, legs, and feet. I chase several grasshoppers before making my first catch. It is an accident and a triumph of frustrated determination when I scare one of them enough so that it flies wildly into the side of the mailbox and knocks itself silly. I clamp my hand over it and tear it from the ground. Clover, grass, dirt and all. I throw it into the jar.

The grasshopper falls to the bottom of the jar and is motionless until I screw down the lid. Then it goes haywire. Hurtling into the glass like a spring let loose. Popping and pinging. Ricocheting like a bullet. I shake the jar with as much force as I can until it drops to the bottom and is still. Its antennae twitch and waver. It stares with black, steely eyes. A brown drop of distress beads at its mouth.

In the ditch, I'm just tall enough to look out over the road. I see birds in the Oxfords' yard, but none of them are at the feeders. Robins on power lines. Starlings in the lawn. Sparrows lining the eaves. Chickadees bounce through the sky like black-and-white yo-yo's on invisible string.

I see grasshoppers, too. Dozens of them in the tall grass, leaping and jumping. Flicking and flinging. I know I can cross the road and catch a jar full of them. And then Dad and I will have what we need to go fishing. I take a step forward and remember the warning.

"When you get out there, stay away from the Oxford place!"

And this is for good reason. Though I've been in their yard before, picking strawberries and digging worms, it was my last visit to the Oxford place that changed things.

☼

"I hate birds," Mr. Oxford said, as he blasted a sparrow out of the top of an evergreen.

My ears rang. Gunpowder burned my nostrils.

"Hate them!" he snarled.

Pieces of feathered flesh fell from limb to limb to limb. Chickadees, starlings, and robins scattered for cover. Mr. Oxford was drunk and getting drunker. He took a long swig from a tall, green bottle then handed it to me.

"Hold this."

"Why do you hate them?" I asked.

He opened a box of shells.

"The missus loves birds. Loves them! Bird pictures. Bird plates. Bird clocks and lamps. We even got bird sheets!"

A seagull was flying overhead. I hoped he wouldn't see it.

"What kind of gun is that?" I asked, trying to distract him.

He reloaded.

The seagull had flown over and was moving away at a good clip. Mr. Oxford raised the gun and sighted in. I was holding the bottle and could only cover one of my ears. The bullet cracked through the sky. The sound kept going and going and going. My head throbbed. My ears screamed. White feathers fluttered down.

He racked out the empty shell. It whistled past my nose and landed in the grass. He smiled, grabbed the bottle from my hand and took another big drink. I watched his Adam's apple bob up and down, up and down, until he finished it. He burped and let the bottle drop to the ground.

"This here is a Model 94 Winchester thirty-thirty. Had it since I was a kid. I'm about the best shot in the world with this gun."

Suddenly, we could hear Mrs. Oxford. She had opened the kitchen window and was yelling from inside.

"Stop shooting birds, you idiot!"

Mr. Oxford's face flushed red. His eyes grew wide. He ran to the window.

"I'll shoot *all* the goddamned birds! Just watch!"

Mr. Oxford turned and ran toward the bushes and trees. He racked and fired, racked and fired, and the birds raced for the clouds. He missed nearly all of them, but blasted a few. The bodies burst like little fireworks. Made bloody, feathered stars and streaks in the sky. Mrs. Oxford wailed, and I high-tailed it toward home, crossed the road, dove into the ditch, and crawled onto my belly.

✿

And now I'm in the ditch again. Picking grasshoppers because I want to go fishing, but it's a task more difficult than I had imagined. All I have is one grasshopper kicking around in a coffee jar. There are others, but they are forbidden. Flying around in the Oxfords' front yard.

From where I stand I can see into the Oxfords' house. Smooth living room shapes and bright colors behind window glass. A quiet house on a quiet street. The Oxfords are nowhere in sight. Everything feels calm. But as I take the steps to cross the road, I hear them. And suddenly, they are at it again.

Mr. Oxford is drunk, charging into the living room. His gun in hand.

"I'll drink if I want to drink!"

Mrs. Oxford follows him, shouting.

"You're crazy! Put that gun away, you idiot! You'll hurt yourself!"

"You don't care! All you care about are those damned birds!"

Mr. Oxford runs to the window and pounds the glass with the butt of the gun. Birds rush into the sky. Mrs. Oxford hurries to the window. Pushes him aside. And puts her big hands on the glass. She watches in horror as the last bird flies. He shoves the gun into her back. She falls to her knees and screams so loud for so long I feel it in my bones. There is no muzzle flash. There is no shot. Instead, he gazes out the window until our eyes meet. Then he pulls the gun away from her and swings the barrel around to his forehead. Slowly, he stretches his fingers toward the trigger.

The gunshot cracks like a thunder clap and sinks deep inside me. I kneel in the grass. My chest pounds. The grasshopper jumps and hammers against the glass. I unscrew the cap, tip the jar onto its side, but the grasshopper clings to wilting grass and dying clover, so I shake the jar as hard as I can until the grasshopper falls out and flies away.

saving turtles

☼

Pink afro wig. Right half of his outfit orange, left half blue. The whole baggy clown suit pulled together over his bony frame by big yellow buttons. Baxter the Clown stood barefoot at the intersection of Grant and Ripley Streets. No painted face. No big red nose. He was a skinny, sick-looking man in a clown suit. I knew his name because he was holding a sign.

BAXTER THE CLOWN
WILL ENTERTAIN
FOR A RIDE NORTH

The stop light was red, so I opened my window. The sky was overcast. The air guaranteed another hot, muggy day.

Baxter the Clown was smiling like a madman.

"Where you headed?" I asked.

Baxter lowered his sign then stepped alongside my truck.

"Anywhere up 23 North. Eventually, to Turtle Lake."

I looked him over. Dirty, yellow fingernails. Stubble-covered cheeks. That bright clown suit.

"I'm not going that far. Ending at Manitou Shores."

"Need some entertainment?" Baxter asked.

"No. But you're welcome to ride."

Baxter jogged around to the passenger side. He jumped in and offered his hand.

"Baxter Wells, transient clown."

His thin, bony hand was strong.

"Aden Wilcox, hung-over fisherman."

Baxter took off his wig. Set it on his lap. On top of the sign he'd been holding. He was bald and had scabs on his head.

The traffic light turned green, but it didn't matter. The intersection was stopped with everyone looking our way. When the light went yellow, I rolled onto Ripley Street. People stared. Mouths opened wide.

"Good fishing at Manitou Shores," Baxter said.

"If you're fishing."

"Isn't that what you're going to do?"

My guts flip-flopped, still aching and sour from Absolut, Budweiser, and sleeping pills.

"I've caught slab perch and twenty pound walleye off Carson's Point," I lied.

Baxter smiled.

"On minnows, right?"

"Yeah, or drifting with crawlers. You fish it much?"

"As a kid I did. My aunt and uncle stayed there a few weeks each summer. My brother and I would stay with them. Uncle Ted would get all liquored up and take us. We'd fish until he conked out. And the ones we caught we let flop all over him while he was unconscious on the floor. Our Aunt Agnes loved it! We'd get the boat back to shore and she'd be soused too, bobbling a camera, taking pictures of him like is was some great event. Him drooling all over himself, covered in fish that were dead or dying."

"Sounds like a great childhood memory," I said, as I turned onto

23 North.

Baxter kept talking.

"Probably more than you wanted to know, but I've lived long enough and pushed through enough shit in life to know that a man ought to just say what he feels, no matter what."

"Well Baxter, I feel like shit."

"Why's that?"

"I tried drinking myself to death last night."

He was quiet, but only for a moment. He wasn't shocked, offended, or disturbed. This clown had seen it all.

"That explains why you're picking up a dirty old clown."

Baxter turned sideways on the seat. He leaned against the door. I was worried he'd fall out.

"The latch on that door isn't too slick, Baxter. I don't know if I'd be leaning on it."

"What do you care?" Baxter asked, smiling. "Why would someone who wants to drink himself to death care what happens to a clown?"

"If I was going to kill myself, I'd have done it. I was only feeling down because my ex-wife..."

"Don't tell me."

Baxter turned and faced the road ahead.

"It doesn't matter. Wife. Job. Money. Trouble with the law. Can't get a hard-on. Whatever. None of it matters."

Baxter was sounding more like a preacher than a clown. I didn't want to talk about it and was sorry I'd brought it up. He kept going.

"None of it matters because it's life. Be a clown. Be a husband. Be a wife. Be a drunk. None of it matters because we're supposed to keep crossing roads. We're supposed to keep moving on."

"I'm not a drunk. I just drink too much sometimes."

Baxter turned around and looked into the bed of the truck.

"You always take concrete blocks and rope when you go fishing?"

"Those are part of a project I was working on."

"The rope's still in the package."

"I didn't need it."

"You're right. You *don't* need it."

The drive was going to be about an hour. One long hour with one talkative clown. When I saw the sign for Jimmie's Liquors, I pulled into the parking lot.

"You drink?" I asked.

Baxter reached into his pocket and pulled out a big, red nose. He put it on and grinned.

"How do you think we end up with these?"

I walked into Jimmie's knowing I'd need at least a 12-pack. Six beers to get the boat out far enough. Six more to tie myself up and go overboard. The problem was I didn't know how much the clown could drink. From the looks of him, I was betting he could put them away. That he *had* been putting them away. And not showering. Maybe even pissing his clown pants. A clown on a bender, I thought.

I thumped a 30-pack of Milwaukee's Best down on the counter. The cashier, a thin, sleepy looking girl, was staring out the window at

Baxter. He'd put on his wig and was smiling and waving, giving the girl the thumbs-up.

"Is that a clown?" she asked.

I took out money to pay, and then squinted out the window like I was trying to see something that wasn't there.

"What clown?" I asked.

"Isn't that a clown in your truck?"

I stepped toward the window and squinted harder. Baxter waved like a nut and bounced in the seat.

"I'm sorry. I don't see anything."

The girl waved to Baxter as she handed me the change.

"That sure looks like a clown," she said.

I took the beer and walked out.

✿

Baxter downed two beers then settled into a steady act of sipping.

"What are you doing in a clown suit, anyway?"

"It's my uniform. I work at Turtle Lake Casino."

I knew Turtle Lake, a small town northwest of the Mackinac Bridge by about two hours. It was home to the popular, ever-expanding Turtle Lake Casino and Resort. It had more RV parks and hotels than houses.

"What do you do there?" I prodded.

"I save lives."

I gulped my beer hoping Baxter would say more about being a clown, about saving lives, but he only chuckled and took off the wig and the nose. I finished my beer and opened another. He took my empty and threw it on the floor.

"A life saver. That figures."

Baxter drank and looked out the window.

"I save turtles, not people, so you're probably fucked."

"Are clowns supposed to swear?"

"Are men supposed to kill themselves?"

We were quiet for miles, but I knew it wouldn't last. Two men in a truck, drinking. Sooner or later, one of us had to talk. Baxter belched and must have known how foul it smelled because he opened his window.

"The center of life is about location and timing," he began. "Like my job. On one side of the road there's Big Bay de Noc. On the other side, behind the casino, you have a thick wooded swamp. Throughout the spring and summer, hundreds of turtles try crossing the road. It's my job to save them. To patrol the road and driveways to make sure turtles aren't getting killed. People unhappy from seeing dead turtles don't generally put a lot of money in the slots."

"But why the suit?"

"I didn't want to be Superman. And that was the only other choice. I don't like capes. Besides, I can't imagine the man of steel walking the roadside, searching for turtles. Too much bending. Sometimes you gotta get right down there on your hands and knees. Can you see Superman doing that?"

I shook my head and took another drink. Baxter went on.

"A clown? That's a different story. Clowns can do anything. You see a clown crouched on the side of the road picking up turtles, it's easier to believe."

The tires hummed. Bugs exploded on the glass. Warm air rushed into the cab smelling like fresh-cut grass. Despite the beer buzz and Baxter's company, I was starting to feel pretty low. Empty and indifferent. And I started to think about it. About how killing myself didn't matter much because we all lived lives of dying, and no matter what we did, where we came from, or what we wanted to be, we were all headed to the same place and there wasn't anything any of us could do about it. And that's when we passed over a turtle that was squashed into the road.

"To dead turtles," Baxter said, raising his beer.

I nodded, raised my beer and drank.

"That doesn't happen when I'm on the job," Baxter said, taking another healthy pull from his can.

He turned to me. His dirty face was solemn. I was glad he wasn't wearing makeup because he would have been the saddest clown I'd ever seen.

"People don't like seeing dead turtles," he said. "Dead skunks. Dead coons. Even dead deer are okay. But you show a person a dead turtle and see what they do. They hate it."

I focused on the road, and I drove.

"Did you know that every year half-a-dozen people get killed trying to save turtles? People driving with direction, going about life, when all of the sudden they see a turtle stretching its neck and slugging its shell across the road. Before you know it, they're jamming on brakes and making U-turns on hairpin curves because they want to save the little bastard."

Baxter paused for another drink. I stared ahead and watched the sun burn away the overcast sky.

"Next thing they know, they're getting ass-packed by the tractor trailer they forgot was behind them, or blind-sided by a car speeding around the corner. It's ugly."

I checked my rearview mirror. Nothing but sunshine and the open road. What Baxter had said sounded fine and true. We opened more beers, drank like fools, and I started feeling like I could drive all day. Me, Baxter, and Milwaukee's Best cruising up 23 North. Men with direction. Meant for places. Feeling better with each passing mile

"BOX TURTLE!" Baxter yelled. "Stop, the truck!"

He got out. Chugged his beer. Threw the empty into the truck bed. He put on his wig, picked up his sign, and shut the door without saying another word. I watched him coax the turtle off the road, onto the gravel shoulder, like a parent with a child. He followed the turtle into the steep ditch. I sat and I drank. And I watched. Until Baxter sank away into the tall, reedy grass.

I looked into the bed of the truck for his beer can but could only see concrete blocks and rope. I checked the rearview mirror once more to make sure there was nothing behind, then I drove ahead to Manitou Shores.

Hotels, cottages, cabins. VACANCY on signs, but places filling fast as tourists unloaded cars and carried luggage. Out-of-state plates. Florida, Texas, Ohio. From Vermont, a giant SUV with dark metallic paint shining under the Michigan sun. Its doors wide open and a picture-perfect family unloading vacation needs. Golf clubs slung over his shoulder. A suitcase in her hands. Two children following. A boy lugging along a blue inflatable alligator. A girl bright and free in a yellow sun dress, wearing orange water-wings. Swimming through the air after her brother, tugging at the alligator's tail. The boy ran, and the girl ran after. He tripped and fell, bounced off the alligator and knocked his head against the sidewalk. The mother dropped the suitcase and ran to the boy. She checked his head, then grabbed the girl by the arm and shook her. The man walked ahead of them. Carried his clubs into the lake front cabin. And shut the door.

Creeping along in tourist traffic, I drove past the family and past Manitou Shores. I drove by great lengths of sandy beach with the Lake

Huron breeze rushing into me. It was the cleanest air I had breathed since I was a kid, and suddenly, I was thinking of something I'd forgotten.

My parents used to take me and my brothers to the beach. We'd spend the day walking the shoreline, scanning the ground for treasures. Shells, spare change, and smooth pebbles. Collecting driftwood. Examining marks in the sand. From birds, dogs, turtles and crabs.

Me and my brothers writing our names in the sand - *Aden, Alex, Anthony*. Dad drawing smiley faces and stick bodies under our names. And Mom drawing a big heart all around it. Around us.

We knew that the water would rise and wash our marks away. That our lines would become smooth and formless underwater. We knew this because one day we stood silent and watched it happen. First, the big heart disappeared. Then the smiley-faced stick bodies. And finally, our names. And somehow it had made things feel important and lasting.

I didn't know why, but as I remembered and things felt sure and solid in my veins, I pulled off 23 North and watched the sun shine on the big lake. An old man and a boy. In a small boat. On the waves. Surrounded by birds. Seagulls, ducks, terns. The man and boy had several loaves of bread. And they were feeding the birds. Tearing pieces away. Throwing them into the water. The birds soared and circled and ate until the bread was gone and the boat moved away. The birds landed and trailed. Bobbed atop the waves. And I watched until all of them were gone. Shapeless and blue. Dissolved by the horizon.

Out of the driver's seat, I stood and stretched. No tourists. No traffic. Only fresh air and the sound of Lake Huron finding the shore. I tied the rope to the block and dragged it through the sand. The wind pushed. Waves rolled hard and crashed white against deep blue. My arms and legs burned and my veins pounded as blood flooded deep into tissues I'd forgotten.

I stepped into the water. Minnows flickered silver as they scattered into the deep. I planted my feet firmly in the sand underwater and held fast to the rope as I lifted the block and swung it around in the air. My body made tight circles. Sand, water, sun. Sand, water, sun. Sand, water, sun. Until the block was weightless, my hands were free, and I was the center of everything.

black bass bay

✪

We were in Grand Lake. Black Bass Bay. Casting Jitterbugs.

The water shimmered silver under the fading sun. Jessie was fishing off the bow. Slinging his line toward a cluster of dark stumps. I fished from the stern. Throwing my line along a weed bed. We'd been at it for two hours. Now, night was coming on and black flies were swarming.

"Need some bug juice?" Jessie asked, dousing his huge arms and legs with repellant. Three years had passed, but it was obvious he hadn't eased off the weights since college.

"No thanks, Jess. I'm good."

Flies buzzed all around me. But they did not land and they did not bite. Before I'd left the house, Sarah had lathered me up with some of her moisturizer.

✪

"Wear this and bugs will leave you alone," she said.

"But I'll smell like a girl."

"Which is better than what you'll smell like when you get back. Beer. Worms. Fish guts."

"I don't think we'll be keeping any."

"Why not?"

"I don't want to gut them."

"I'm sure the brute will do it."

"He's not a brute, Sarah."

She frowned. Turned away. Went to the kitchen and came back

with the cooler.

"Six beers. That's all. Okay?"

"We probably won't even drink that many," I said.

Sarah stood in front of me. Put her head against my chest.

"I don't understand why you're doing this."

"We were best friends, Sarah."

"*Were*," she said. "A lot has changed since college. Now, you have nothing in common."

"We have lots in common."

"God, I hope not."

She pulled away.

"He's not a bad guy, Sarah."

"He's not a good guy, either," she said. "He's all testosterone and machismo."

"And you like the soft feminine type?"

"I love them," she said.

And she leaned in and kissed me.

☼

Half an hour before the cabin, I'd opened a beer. Sipped it and wondered how it would be. Our first meeting since our falling out. Three years ago. At a party. After the championship. When we were celebrating because Jessie, our defensive captain, had forced a fumble, recovered the ball and won the game. Celebrating because we were seniors. Young men with potential. A whole world to conquer. Full of piss and vinegar. Hell bent on catching our dreams.

I was stumbling drunk through the party. Trophy full of beer under my arm. Searching for Jessie.

"Where's the hero?" I asked everybody I bumped into. "We gotta drink from the trophy!"

The last anybody saw of him he was headed down the basement stairs with a fresh keg on his shoulder.

"Where's the goddamned hero?" I shouted, as I moved down the stairs. Beer sloshing around in the trophy. Steadying myself against the wall.

✿

I reeled and watched the shoreline. A blue heron stalked the shallows. Swallows skimmed the water. Chickadees chanted. Squirrels scampered through branches.

I heard a splash and turned just in time to see a big bass slip into the water behind my lure.

"Slow on the draw," I said.

Jessie reached into the cooler. Took out a beer and tossed it to me.

"Drink up. It'll help your reflexes."

Another bass jumped. Near the stumps. Jessie cast his Jitterbug into the ripples it left behind.

I reeled in. Sat down. Opened the beer and sipped. My eyes were drawn to a place on the shoreline. Something ran through the trees.

"I'm glad you came," Jessie said.

He reeled in. Sat down.

"I know this must seem pointless to you," he said. "But I'm sorry."

He raised his beer. Gestured a toast.

I nodded. Raised my beer.

"To friends," I said.

"Goddamn right," Jessie said. "To friends."

✿

There were two doors in the basement. At the bottom of the stairs. One was open to a room filled with people hovering around a keg. Talking. Laughing. Dancing. Jessie wasn't among them. I moved to the other door. Someone had hung a DO NOT DISTURB sign over the doorknob.

"Jessie! You in there?"

I pounded on the door.

There was no answer.

"Jessie! You sonofabitch! Open the door! We gotta drink from the trophy!"

I thought I heard a girl laughing. Hysterically.

"Jessie! You goddamned hero! You better not be..."

I stumbled forward. Fell into the door. And it opened.

The girl's hands were tied awkwardly behind her back. She was on her belly. Skirt and panties around her knees. And Jessie was on her. His hand over her mouth. Holding her down.

"Get out!" he shouted. "Get out!"

☼

The sun was nearly gone. Dropping down orange. Behind the treetops. Jessie had closed his eyes and was resting. He took a deep breath. Savored it. Exhaled slowly, as if it was the best breath he'd ever taken.

I closed my eyes. Listened to his breathing and to the sound of bass breaking the surface of the black water, and beyond it, near the shoreline, I heard something else. A struggle. A splash. Something heavy in the water.

Jessie was up, pointing toward the shore.

"Do you see that?"

There was a large gray dog at the shoreline. Pacing back and forth. And there was a deer in the water. Swimming out toward Grand Island, which was a quarter mile away.

"She's not gonna make it," Jessie said, and he grabbed an oar.

"What are you doing?"

"We gotta help," he said.

"Why don't we use the motor?"

"She's already in a panic," he said. "The motor will make it worse."

He pulled a rope out from under his seat and he threw it to me.

"Make a big loop," he said. "If it looks like she's going under, throw it around her neck and we'll pull her toward shore."

I tied the loop and held tight to the rope. He rowed us. And we moved quietly across the water. Into the coming darkness. Following her.

the horn

✿

The snow had been coming all day. First in flurries. Then in steady, heavy wet flakes. It was good packing snow, so I was making snowballs and throwing them at the cows. Not throwing to hit them, but to see how they'd react. The only one that paid any attention was Cybil, the old white cow. But she only stared at me as the snowballs landed all around her. Her big dark eyes unblinking. It looked liked someone had walked out into the field and made a cow out of snow. The other cows had their heads buried in hay. Each of them wearing white blankets of snow on their backs. At five, when Tom's Chevette came sliding into the driveway, Cybil put her head down and walked over to the others.

I got in the car. Stomped the snow off my feet.

"Why ya gotta bring all that snow in here?" Tom asked.

"If you haven't noticed, it's a goddamned blizzard out there."

"You could've stomped off outside."

"In the snow? What good would that do?"

Tom's face was wind burned. He was wearing a red-and-black checkered hunting hat. It had long hanging earflaps and a drooping brim. He had the strings of the earflaps tied up under his orange beard.

"You owe five bucks."

"For what?"

"Beer."

"What beer?"

Tom reached over the seat and came away with two bottles of Pabst. We popped off the tops with our seatbelts and clanked the bottles together.

"Cheers," Tom said.

I looked out the window at Cybil. She was chewing. Watching us

go.

"To Cybil," I said.

"I'm not drinking to a cow."

"Why not?"

"Because, she'll be steak before too long."

"Cybil's a milker. Not an eater."

Tom spun us around in a donut then headed us out of the driveway. The snow was piling up like mad, coming down so heavily that Tom had us slowed to a crawl.

"Fucking snow," he said.

"Where'd you get the beer?"

"From Stan."

"Stan Kowalski?"

"Yep, Stan the man."

"How'd you convince him to buy for us?"

"I gave him Emily Thompson's number."

"But you don't even know her number."

Tom turned on the headlights. Cranked up the heat. The Chevette's engine sputtered.

"I know, but everyone thinks that you two had a thing, and since I am your best friend..."

"We did NOT have a thing," I said. "It was one date."

"Whatever. I made up a number. Said it was Emily's and that I got it from you."

"You're an asshole, Tom."

"Thanks, buddy!"

He smiled. Raised his bottle for a toast. We chugged away at the bottles and raced to the bottoms.

"Where do you want the empties?" I asked.

"Save 'em for the horn."

I put the bottles on the floor between my feet.

Tom turned us left onto Oldfield Street. We fish-tailed around the corner. Opened two more bottles.

✿

Tom and I had always traveled like this. Weekend, weeknight. Summer, spring, winter, fall. We'd hop into his Chevette and drive the horn. A rough stretch of roads that ran off behind the Clifton Cement Plant, alongside Misery Bay, through swampy lowlands teeming with cedars and evergreens, then back up to higher ground where there were farms and apple orchards. We called it the horn because halfway into our trip there was this driveway with a big, red ship horn at the end of it, and when we neared it, I'd take whatever empties were handy, lean out the window, and see how many I could throw into the opening. It wasn't easy because Tom would either speed up or slow down and swerve all over so I couldn't get my timing right. My record was three bottles in the hole. But more often than not, the bottles ended up shattering against the horn and the pieces fell into the driveway. It didn't matter, Tom said, because the place was only a summer cottage. Owned by some hi-tech CEO from Grosse Pointe.

Tom and I drank a lot for a couple of kids. It wasn't a big deal for each of us to drink ten or twelve beers while cruising the horn. I never drove. Tom always did. The fact that his dad was an ex-lawyer turned mayor, and that my dad worked at the cement plant had a bit to do with that. Tom's Dad would bail him out if he got busted for drunk driving, whereas mine would have beat my ass. Dad didn't care so much that I drank, but he swore to God he'd kill me if I ever got caught drunk driving, and I never argued the point because Dad had his reason.

It was two days before Christmas. Mom was on her way home from Fishers Big Wheel with a carload of gifts. And Willie Lunker hit her head on. From what the paper had said, Willie had worked the midnight shift and four hours of overtime, then stopped at The Corner Bar for a half-dozen beers or so. He killed my mom with his Dodge Ram in the early afternoon as she waited at a stoplight. I've seen the newspaper clipping. Our blue Plymouth station wagon crumpled up into a wad of metal. Fishers Big Wheel bags, new toys and clothing, spread over the pavement. The only thing that made Mom's death real was the caption.

Scene of the crash, which claimed the life of 24 year old Alpena woman, Tabitha Kausabowski.

✿

I grabbed two more beers out of the backseat.

"Let's see if we can finish a few more of these before we get to the horn," Tom said.

I opened the beers and handed him one.

"What's the hurry?" I asked.

"This weather's a bitch. If we get stranded out here it'd be nice to have a good buzz on."

The shoreline of Lake Huron was white. The sky was white. The Chevette trudged along, pushing snow like a miniature plow. I could hear the car's bottom scraping along the drifts and feel the snow pounding against the floorboards. Tom steered with his knees. I reached down to turn on the radio.

"Don't turn that on."

"Why not?"

"Because, the less we got going, the less likely this thing will stall. I got the heat on and that's plenty. In fact..."

Tom reached over and turned down the heat.

"We can't turn on the radio?"

"No, we got the headlights on and the heat on low. That's enough."

"That's crazy. The radio's not gonna stall the car."

"You wanna chance it and end up pushing?"

I sipped at my beer.

The road, its shoulders, and the ditches were gone. Everything

68

was lost beneath the snow. The windshield was beginning to fog, so Tom switched the blower from heat to defrost.

"Aren't you afraid that sudden change in power is gonna stall us?"

He shot me a sideways glance.

"Go to hell, smartass."

"You're the one that's going to hell, Tom. Lying to Stan about Emily's number."

"Emily...what a dame, hey?"

"She's all right."

"So, what happened on your date?"

"Nothing."

"Don't give me that shit. What happened?"

I drank more beer.

"Fine," Tom said. "You don't want to talk. That's fine. I pick you up every day. Get the beer. Pay for the gas. Drive us around. And *still* you can't tell me what happened with Emily."

"A gentleman never tells."

"Tells what? You said nothing happened."

I tried to look out over Misery Bay, but I couldn't see. I wondered if anyone had put their shanties out yet, and if they had, I wondered if the ice would be thick enough to hold a man, his shanty, and all of the snow.

"Your old man put his shanty out yet?" I asked.

"Don't change the subject."

Tom reached over the seat and grabbed two more beers. The Chevette kept on plowing through snow.

The horn was hardly ever plowed. The people who lived along these roads owned summer and winter cars. Sports cars and sleek sedans for the steady, warm months. Sport utility vehicles for the cold unpredictable months. Some of these folks even owned an extra truck, an old Dodge Ram or a Chevy Silverado. They were full-size and four-wheel-drive, with tires bigger than they needed to be, and usually they were outfitted with a winch and a plow. These trucks were used for "knocking around," as I'd heard them say. For towing fishing boats and motorbikes, for going to camp, and for keeping the pavement of their wide, winding driveways clear.

I thought of my Dad driving home in his old Ford F-150, the only vehicle he'd owned since the Plymouth he and Mom shared, and I knew that with all the snow he'd be out plowing tonight. He would go home. Shower. Eat. Then take care of his regulars that called. Jesse from Woody's Market, wanting the driveway plowed. Reverend Jenkins from Hope Lutheran Church, praying for a cleared parking lot. Old people on the outskirts of town that wanted to be able to make it to the mailbox. And a few single mothers that always called, afraid of being snowed in because they could never tell when one of their kids would get sick or hurt. Sometimes, Dad said these women invited him in. For coffee, cocoa, dinner. But Dad always respectfully declined.

Tonight, Dad would eat the stew I'd made. Beef stew with carrots, potatoes, and mushrooms. Left simmering atop the woodstove, it would fill the house with flavor. And Dad would smile. Be happy that I'd remembered him. Thought of him. That I was kind enough to leave a note saying, "Went riding the horn with Tom. Checking for shanties."

Tom stopped the car and started to get out.

"What are you doing?" I asked.

"I gotta piss."

"You're just gonna leave the car here in the middle of the road?"

"Ease up. Nobody'll be down this way for another half hour. Not in this weather, anyway."

Tom slammed the door and jogged off into a stand of pines. I watched him until he vanished into the sagging snow-covered boughs.

I reached down and turned on the radio. The car shuddered. There was nothing but static, so I shut it off and sat there thinking about Emily Thompson and the date we'd had.

It had been a cold day. But nice and clear, and Emily had said she wanted to have a picnic. There was snow on the ground. So I didn't believe her until I pulled into her driveway and she walked out of her house with a cooler and a backpack.

"What's in the cooler?"

I tried to take it from her, and offered to take the pack, but she refused.

"It's a surprise, mister. You just keep your hands off."

I went around and opened the trunk. Shoved aside the spare tire, my fishing gear and my rifle to make room for the cooler.

"You *hunt*?" she asked.

"I just like being outdoors, I guess."

"Sure, that's what they all say. Killing poor, helpless animals. You're all brutes, as far as I'm concerned."

I closed the trunk. She smiled and got in the passenger side.

Fresh-faced. Brown-eyed. Silky black hair. Shiny pink lip gloss. Emily was so pretty she looked out of place. Everywhere. At school. At parties. At the mall. And on that day, in my old car that was filled with blankets, jumper cables, empty bottles, snow bibs, a bag of sand, a shovel, and my own cooler. Full of fish because I'd been fishing for bluegill that morning and hadn't had time to go home. I hadn't showered or shaved. I was wearing Sorels, a quilted flannel, and a knitted hat. And as we rode out into the sunny fresh, snow-covered country, and she talked about moving to Chicago to go to medical school, I wondered why she'd agreed to go out with me.

We'd been in the car driving and talking for about an hour before we stopped.

"This is good," she said. "I like this place. It's pretty. What do you call it?"

"Hempel's Mill."

"Why's it called that?"

"I'm not sure. I think it used to be a saw mill. You know, logging and stuff. In fact, if I'm not mistaken, this path we're on is an old logging trail. See how it dips down there to the stream?"

Emily unbuckled her seatbelt and leaned forward. She stared down to the place where the stream bubbled through the ice. My heater didn't work and she looked cold, so I was surprised when she unbuttoned her coat.

"You warm?" I asked.

"Very," she said.

She slipped out of her coat and tossed it into the backseat. Something fell from a pocket and onto the floor.

"What's that?" I asked.

"It's my cell phone. Never know when I'm going to need it, especially when parked in the woods with strange boys."

She smiled. Leaned over to pick up the phone. Put her hand on my thigh.

"Use it much?" I asked.

"Only in emergencies," she said.

She glanced back at the stream.

"It's an awfully small stream for logging."

"It used to be bigger. Wider. Since the cement plant put up their hunting club back in the woods, the water's slowed to a trickle here. Rumor has it that they've redirected the stream so that it flows through their property."

"Oh, it's not a rumor. It's true. I've seen it. I've stood in it. Up to my knees, trying to catch crayfish. My Dad and his buddies are always out there drinking beer and playing cards. Sometimes I go back there to play with them. I'm surprised you've never been back there. Your dad works at the plant, doesn't he?"

I pictured her white collar Dad and the rest of his cronies. Wearing khakis and weekend hikers, drinking imported beer, and talking about how they would head out at the crack of nine to make a killing, trolling Lake Huron with down-riggers, depth-finders, and navigational systems on their boats named *Money Talks* or *Dollar's Wake*. And right then I knew that I wanted nothing to do with Emily Thompson. Not a picnic, not a conversation, not anything. And that's how I worked up the nerve to lean into her and give her pink glossy lips a try.

☼

Tom jumped into the car. Snow whirled in behind him. His eyes were wide. He had a big grin plastered across his face.

"You're not going to believe what I just saw!"

"What?"

"A big, fat, hound with a bell around it's neck!"

"In this? Are you nuts? Nobody's running a dog in this."

"Man, I know what I saw!"

"I think you better lay off the sauce, Tom."

"It was a hound wearing a bright, red collar! And it had a bell around its neck, and it was jingling!"

"You sound like a nut, Tom. Calm down."

He sat and looked all around out the windows.

"We should go out and find him!"

"What for?"

"We could probably stick one of these Lake Huron rich pricks for a reward, that's why!"

"Tom, you're losing it. It's a dog. It's probably halfway home by now. You probably scared the shit out of it when you stomped into the woods."

"Come on, let's go!"

"No way! I thought we were gonna just drive the horn and drink, and that's what I came to do. Besides, it's cold out and the wind's really starting to blow. Drifts are getting higher and if we go traipsing through the woods we might end up lost. And I'm not freezing my ass off for some dog."

Tom shook his head.

"That's just it. You always got your head up your ass. Anytime some great opportunity comes along like this, you shirk it off. Like Emily. I bet you didn't even kiss her, did you?"

Both of us were quiet for a minute. We drank and listened to the wind as it blew up off the lake and screamed around the car. I could feel the Chevette rocking in the gusts.

"It's not letting up any. Maybe we should head back," I said.

"No, we're almost to the horn. Besides you still haven't told me about Emily."

"There's nothing to tell."

Tom leaned back in his seat. Steered with his knees.

"You should've seen that hound. Pushing his nose through drifts! Bell ringing! It was the prettiest thing I ever saw!"

We drank more and moved alongside Misery Bay. I tried to look out my window and see shanties, but the glass was steamed up. Just like it was when I was with Emily.

✡

Emily's body pressed hard against mine. Her mouth was hot. Everything - the windows, the steering wheel, our bodies - was steaming. Her hand fought my zipper, and I wondered if she realized that I still had my seatbelt on. I tried to unbuckle it so I could take off my coat, but by the time I had one arm out of its sleeve, Emily had unbuttoned her shirt and was shoving her naked breasts into my face. They smelled like oranges and baby powder. So strong, I could barely breathe.

"You want me, don't you?" she whispered.

All of it - the heat, Emily's pawing, and the seatbelt holding me down - was suffocating. I eased back into my seat. Gently lifted her away so I could catch my breath and unbuckle my seatbelt. And all of the sudden she stopped and glared at me.

"What's wrong?" she asked.

"My seatbelt..."

She leaned back against the steering wheel. Covered herself with her arms.

"Is it me?"

"No, I was just..."

I reached for her, but she shoved me back against the seat.

"You think I'm a whore, don't you?"

"No. Not at all. I was just trying to unbuckle my seatbelt."

"All you fucking guys think I'm a whore! That's why you ask me out! That's why you all drive me out to some fucking trail in the woods!"

She moved to reach for her shirt and hit her head on the rearview mirror. Tears flooded her eyes. She scrambled to her seat, snatched up her phone and began to dial.

"What are you doing?"

"If you don't get us out of here and take me home this instant, I'm calling my father!"

Without another word between us, I started the car, backed us out of Hempel's Mill and raced us back toward her house.

We didn't say anything on the way back. Not even when I ran over a cottontail that jumped into the road. There was only the sound of my old car. The engine chugging. Fan belt squealing. Tires crunching against snow. And that rabbit. Thumping against the floorboards before flopping off onto the side of the road to die.

When we got to her place, she was out of the car and headed into her house before I was even able to remind her to take her backpack and cooler.

I thought about keeping her stuff, but I knew better. Eventually, I would have to see her again, and things had gone wrong enough already. So I grabbed her backpack, her cooler, and set them inside her old man's Land Rover. But I made sure to open them first, so that he could see her stash of condoms, the six-pack of beer and the fifth of whiskey she'd brought. With all that done, I looked at the sky and was thankful that it was still clear and light because that meant there was still plenty of time to go fishing with Tom.

✿

Tom tossed his empty bottle into my lap and it startled me.

"We're almost there. Get ready."

I opened the window. Stuck a bottle on each finger of my left hand and held another one in my right. I turned sideways in the seat and leaned out into the snow. The wind felt like icy knives and I could hardly breathe as snow rushed in all around me.

"Can't you block some of that shit from blowing in here?" Tom yelled.

"Just keep her steady!"

My eyes were watering like crazy and I blinked again and again to keep them from freezing. I could barely see the big red horn through the swirling snow.

"How many bottles you got?" Tom asked.

"One in the barrel and five in the chamber!"

I dangled out the window and readied my aim. I could feel the cold slicing through me. Hitting bone. And I could hear Tom yelling something, but it was drowned by the sound of wind in my ears.

We were about twenty yards from the horn when I let the first bottle go. It veered off to the right and was sucked away into the white. I reloaded quickly and threw two more. Both of them sailed over the horn and disappeared. Tom was yelling something to me again and suddenly the car was swerving all over the road. I dropped two of the bottles down the side of the car, and as I struggled to get the last one off my thumb, Tom hit the brakes. The Chevette jumped and spun. My head slammed into the door frame. Tom wrestled with the steering wheel as bottles, tools, and his fishing gear went airborne all around us. My body lunged forward into the windshield and when I heard glass shattering I closed my eyes.

Tom pounded his fists on the steering wheel.

"Goddammit! Goddammit! Goddammit!"

I pushed myself away from the dashboard. Checked myself over. There was only a small lump on my head.

"Get up!" Tom yelled. "And come on!"

He opened the door and ran down the road. Toward the horn. I got out, steadied myself, and followed. It was hard to run in the snow. And hard to see. My head hurt and my chest hurt. And I didn't know what had happened until I saw Tom kneeling in the road.

Ahead of us, headlights beamed through the snow, but Tom remained there. Hunched over. As if frozen in the middle of a prayer.

"Tom, there's a car coming! Get outta the road!"

I shoved my hands deep into my pockets. Dragged my feet through the heavy drifts. I felt something bad had happened, and that something had been happening since I'd been standing at home, throwing snowballs at Cybil, waiting for Tom to show.

The hound's body was stretched out in the snow. Its eyes were closed and one long ear was flipped back over its head filling up with snow. Tom touched the shiny bell on the dog's collar.

"She won't be running no more," he said.

I knelt beside him. The wind blew up around us. Snow fluttered down the back of my neck and the chill it gave me felt good.

"I don't think that car is gonna see us, Tom. We better get out of the road."

Tom brushed the snow away from the hound's ear. I slid my arms under her and lifted her from the road. Besides a single spot of blood on the snow, all that remained was the imprint of her body.

The headlights neared and three white faces peered through the windshield of a high-riding, black four wheel drive Dodge. It was a young woman with two small children. A boy and a girl. The woman's head dropped. The children's mouths fell open. And I knew that they'd been out a long time. Searching in the storm.

one-legged goose

✿

All suited up in eighty degree heat. Standing in the Alpena Sportsmen's Club. Drinking because I'm hung-over and all I want to do is get through the rest of this thing. The wedding. The reception. The celebration. The party.

People talking all around me. Old friends turned into acquaintances, and I feel like I don't know anybody anymore. Like all of us are faking our way through the night. Through life. Nothing is as it seems. We talk about old times, shake hands, give hugs, and make promises to keep in touch, knowing we never will.

I lean against the bar, knock back my vodka tonic and order another.

All around the place there are green and white decorations. Streamers, flowers, bows. Tablecloths, candles, napkins. It's a nice look. Clean. Crisp. Proper. The bartender fills my cup and slides it across the bar. A green and white sign hangs from the ceiling. It's so big and bright, it's dizzying.

CONGRATULATIONS MIKE AND SARA!

There's cheering in the corner of the room. The bride and groom are shoving cake into each other's face. Laughing. Teasing. Playing it up for the crowd. Loving the moment. Licking frosting. Unaware of a past or a future. Brushing away crumbs. Knowing only Now.

I drink and walk outside.

Some of the old timers are gathered together. Smoking and

drinking. Mumbling and nodding. Standing around a three-foot-tall, iron bear. An impressive, intricate figure whose beauty is lost on functionality. It is an ashtray. Mouth open wide, iron saliva stringing from big, mean, iron teeth with muscles bulging under a smooth iron coat, as powerful arms stretch upward holding an iron bowl of butts and ashes.

I can't look at it for long because all I keep thinking is that it's a damned shame somebody's put so much into making an ashtray.

I turn away from the bear and the old men, and I see my reflection in the window glass. I'm all dressed up. Wide and distorted. Thinning blond hair. Stubby fingers fidgeting and shaking around a plastic cup. My short dark legs are stuck into the concrete, but my body sways. I'm a tired groomsman. A drunken figurine. A man in a suit playing a role in a tradition that is not mine, aware that what I've become is something for someone else to see. I am shadow and light. A minute in the moment. Part of a day of time to be remembered. I'm a body in the background of a snapshot. A flash in someone's memory. Part of the reflection of the world. I'm looking at it. And it is looking at me. And I know there's got to be more to all of it. To all of this. So I look away from what's in front of me.

I stand in the fading daylight and gaze out over the blue-tipped grass toward the pond.

The water's smooth. Swallows sail and loop, turning barrel rolls and skimming the surface. Cattails and lily pads. Evergreens and birch trees. The sky and everything under it reflects and shines in the water like mirrored glass.

I'm thinking about asking the old timers if the pond is stocked with fish, but one of them starts this long, hacking cough, so I keep my trap shut. The raspy hacking turns to gasping breath. The old timer bends over, veins bulging and snaking under his skin, face going red then blue. He is suffocating. I step forward to help, but his buddies raise their hands to stave me off.

"Don't mind Stosh! He does this all the time!"

But by now, Stosh is on one knee. Pounding his chest. Eye to eye with the iron bear. Begging for breath.

One of his friends looks at his watch.

"He has been at it a while."

Stosh pounds his chest some more then starts this deep, lung-rattling growl.

Another buddy pipes up.

"He's pulling out of it!"

I sip my drink and fiddle with my tie. There's drinking, cake eating, merrymaking going on just inside the doorway, but at my feet, a man moves closer to dying.

Seeing this has me feeling light-headed, hot, and just when I think I'm about to pass out and join Stosh, he wretches up the most god-awful, chunk of black phlegm I've ever seen and spits it onto the ground.

One of his buddies slaps him on the back.

"Buck up, Stosh!"

Silvery threads of spittle stretch and hang down from Stosh's purple lips. Watery-eyed and sweating, he wipes his mouth on his sleeve, and he rises.

Before his face can even regain its color, he's giving me a wink, and lighting a cigarette.

"I need a drink!" he hollers.

Another drink sounds fine. I drain my cup and glance inside toward the bar. The band strikes up a real hum-dinger of a tune, and I imagine the dancing's about to rip to life. Soon the place will be hotter than hell, filled with dancing bodies, and people will be moving in ways that are amazing and obscene. Dads shaking hips. Moms gyrating. Grandparents doing the chicken dance.

Watching people is usually my favorite part of a wedding reception, but tonight I don't feel like watching. Maybe it's the hangover within my buzz. Maybe it's the heat. Maybe it's something I don't even know. But what I do know is I'm single, and I'm at a wedding, and I sure as hell don't want to take part in the goddamned garter toss. There's always some fat-assed, ugly broad with the personality of a tree stump just chomping at the bit to catch the damned bouquet, and my idea of fun isn't trying to slide a garter belt up some monster's ham-hock. So when I start to feel like it's nearing garter tossing time, I do my best to avoid the whole situation.

One time, I spent half an hour sitting on a banquet hall toilet, and I didn't even have to go to the bathroom. I just sat there staring at the stall door. FUCK MARRIAGE, it said in thin scratchy letters, and I imagined some pissed off receptionite, drunk off his ass, scratching those words into the metal door, making some sort of bold statement because he had been hurt, because he was jealous, because he was alone. FUCK MARRIAGE, it said, and I thought that was just fine because I can't count how many times I wanted to take my jackknife out of my pocket and scratch FUCK THE GARTER TOSS into a wall, into a door, into a mirror.

Stosh and his buddies are ready to head to the bar, and I'm about to follow when this zillion-year-old sack of bones comes creak-swaying out of the Sportsmen's Club. She's wearing a jet-black wig, about a half-gallon of paint on her face, and she's smiling crazy. The best part is she's wearing this really sexy dress. A purple one that plunges nearly all the way to her bellybutton, showing off tan saggy skin. She's got a plastic champagne glass shaking to hell in one hand and a cigarette burning up in the other.

"Which one of you old bastards is gonna to dance with me?" she shouts.

The old timers hoot and holler and laugh until old Stosh starts hacking again. They stand around him slapping him on the back, telling him to "hang in there" and "buck up," until finally he hacks up another chunk. As he gasps for breath, the purple-dressed bombshell takes him by the arm.

"At least this one won't get away!" she cackles, and then leads him inside.

Stosh's buddies laugh and follow.

When they leave, I feel like all the energy's been knocked out of me. I want to sit down, but there isn't a chair anywhere, so I lean against the building and take deep breaths. I'm 30, but feeling like a 103. My chest feels tight. My face burns. My mouth is stone dry. It's because I've been drinking. It's because I'm tired. Tired of this place. Tired of the phony smiles and cordial bullshit. Tired of tradition and people and everything not being what it seems.

The iron bear's at my feet, so I start looking at it again. I can't get over how detailed it is, how real it looks, but then I realize I've never seen a real bear. I've fished, hunted, camped, and spent hours in the woods, yet I've never seen a real, live bear. It gets me feeling kind of sad because I think maybe the only bear I'll ever see is if I end up going to the zoo some day. And I don't ever want to go to the zoo if I can help it. All those caged animals can't be happy. But maybe I'll have a wife and some kids one day, and I'll have to go to the zoo, just like I'll have to do a million other things I don't want to do. But I hope to hell I can see a real bear before then. That way if I do end up going to the zoo with my kids, I can tell them how good it is to see an animal in the wild. That their old man was a hunter. A fisher. And one day while tracking a whitetail, or setting up camp, or running a trout line, I ran into a bear. A big one. One so big and fearsome that the only thing I could do was stand still and stare it down. It would be a great story. One they could go to school with and tell to their friends. And maybe even tell their own kids one day.

I put my empty cup over the iron bear's snout and walk toward the pond. The sky is doing funny things with color and texture. Treetops are filled with pink light. Thin, wispy clouds are streaked blue and orange. The grass, trampled earlier by the wedding ceremony, has straightened itself out and is reaching toward the sun.

✿

It's hard to believe that only a few hours earlier I was one of the cows trampling the grass. Walking down the makeshift aisle with a pudgy, tree stump bridesmaid on my arm. One that had overdosed on tanning and was looking like a gigantic rotisserie chicken. I was glad I'd hit the bottle first thing in the morning, otherwise I wouldn't have made it through.

"Do you have a girlfriend?" she'd asked, as we readied for our walk.

I was roasting in my suit, feeling I might collapse, and my biggest concern was getting to the reverend at the end. A young, chubby, bearded man in a little motorized cart. No shit. I kid you not. The reverend, the mighty master of love and ceremony, was in a little motorized cart. Like the ones you see at grocery stores. Always lined up and ready to go, but hardly anyone ever using them. I wanted to laugh, probably because deep down I'm a mean bastard, but mostly because it was just crazy. He was so young. So bearded. So chubby. Sitting there, hands on his handlebars, Bible in his lap, smiling at us like we were the husband and wife to be.

It was steaming hot, and I needed a drink. I wanted to sit down. Wanted this thing over, but there I was with an overdone bridesmaid on my arm asking me if I had a girlfriend.

"No, I'm single. Do you?"

"Do I what?" she asked.

"Have a girlfriend?"

Her big, dark, dead-cow eyes came to life. But only for a second.

89

"Do I *look* like a lesbian?"

"I don't know. What does one look like?"

I was trying to be funny, but trying to go deep, too, beyond the reception, our costumes, the way we were supposed to BE, but it wasn't working. I was too tired, a little buzzed up, and sweating like mad.

"Are you *all right?*" she asked.

"I'm fine. How are you?"

"You smell like beer."

"Sorry," I said.

She fell quiet. So did I. We stood and waited for the flutist to start it up. A flutist. The first goddamned wedding ever that had a flutist play the wedding march. A young girl. About 14. Tall and lanky. Her body still deciding whether it wanted to be a boy or a girl, but she had forced the issue and her hair was all done up, and her face was caked in makeup, not wanting at all to be a girl but to be a woman instead. Seeing the flutist helped me forget how uncomfortable I was because I started thinking about her and all the things she probably thinks she's gone through, and all the shit she will go through, and I was feeling connected to her. The way it sometimes is when you just sit and think of someone else for a while.

But then the body on my arm spoke up.

"You really stink! How many drinks do you need to get through a wedding?"

"Seven feels about right."

"Why do I always end up with the losers?"

Now she was just being mean.

"There's no ending up, sister. We're all losers."

That really threw her for a loop.

"Whatever. Can't you just take me down the aisle?"

I'd missed the rehearsal, so I was winging the whole thing. Not that there was much to wing. A walk down the aisle, even when the wedding is outside and there really isn't an aisle, isn't a big deal. I've been walking on two legs since I was a kid. It was being there I should have rehearsed for. Seeing the Sportsmen's Club, the decorations, the young reverend in his motorized cart. And maybe the flute player would have been at the rehearsal too, and I could have seen her. Maybe as a kid being a kid. Not wearing women's hair and women's makeup. Not trying to be anything at all. But sometimes rehearsals and seeing things before they happen isn't a good thing. Sometimes it doesn't matter, so it's best to have a few drinks and let your feet fall where they may.

Mine were walking down the aisle. One foot in front of the other.

My sweetie-pie bridesmaid was holding my arm too tight. She had put on this wide, toothy grin and was winking and waving at people like she was the queen of some damned parade. I tried to forget she was there, and did my best to stay on the straight and narrow, but out of nowhere a little boy ran into the aisle.

He was round-faced. Had curly blond hair. Was wearing a shirt and tie. He'd found a small birch twig and was holding it up toward me, as if it were a gift. No parent or sibling ran to claim him, and I heard a few gasps in the crowd, like the kid was doing something really horrible, so as casually as I could, I stopped and opened my hand. The bridesmaid started playing it up of course, trying to goo-goo talk with the kid, even posing for snapshots people were taking, but this kid was focused on only one thing. Me.

His eyes were deep blue. Eyes that when I looked into them made me stop and feel the inner workings of myself. Like a timepiece becoming aware of its parts. Face on the outside. Guts on the inside. Gears, cogs, and wheels turning, clicking, driving hands on the surface, sweeping them around to tick off time, as if life doesn't matter. And for a few seconds, everything stopped for synchronization. My guts rolled and warmed. My mind lit up, and this little kid had me. Had IT. That something that makes us know there's more to this than meets the eye. He put the birch twig in my hand. Smiled and reached for me to hold him.

My lovely bridesmaid took the twig and tossed it aside. She shook her finger at the boy, "Run along now, honey!" she said.

I thought I was going to be sick when we crossed the finish line, but I wasn't. I stood my ground and waited for the other cows. I searched the crowd for the kid, but when I knew I wouldn't see him again, I turned and stared blindly at the pond, counting the minutes until the open bar.

☼

Now I'm a bit buzzed up, but sort of down and dying, and I'm standing at the edge of the pond. Watching water striders, water beetles, and a doomed dragonfly. On his back, curling his long blue body into a horseshoe and spinning. Another dragonfly is in the air above him, hovering. Waiting, it seems. I crouch down to get a better look, and a frog leaps into the water. It's long-legged and sleek and glides under the surface until it disappears into the shadows of the lily pads. The hovering dragonfly rockets away. The one in the water stops still, laid out flat against the water. Big eyes watching the wide sky.

I hear something in the grass behind me. I stand and turn to look and I see a one-legged goose. Hopping and balancing. Pecking the ground. The left foot and part of the leg are gone. All that's left is a black nub that cannot reach the ground. It is disturbing and fascinating. Sad but true.

I approach slowly and talk to the one-legged goose.

"It's okay, old boy. Just saying hi."

The goose pecks furiously. Takes in grass, bugs, and seeds. Tosses aside cigarette butts, foil gum wrap, and confetti.

"What happened to you, little fella?"

I'm about as close as I can get. Crouched down an arm's length away when the goose rears its head and takes a shot at me. I'm startled and fall backward. The goose stands tall, hissing. He is all the world's strength balancing on one leg. He hops forward and stretches his wings, and I am able see the rest of his grace. A small deformed wing beating with fury. The goose hisses once more, then is calm. I am still, and I wait. He moves his head side-to-side and looks me over. When he's had his fill of me, he hops away to the edge of the pond. Searches the shoreline and the shallows, as if looking for something, then moves into the water and swims slowly in one-legged circles

He is evolution's answer. The food chain's broken link. A length of leg. A broken wing. A moment of life given to fate. And suddenly, I know there are fish in the pond. I can feel them in the air, sense them in the cool grass, and I know that they are here. Bluegill and bass. Perch and carp. And somewhere below the surface, a northern pike cruises the bottom, goslings deep in its belly. In its blood. Pushing gills in and out.

There is a big splash in the pond, and when I look to the place where the dragonfly floated, it is gone. The surface rings with ripples. The goose honks then struggles to swim straight as it heads toward the opposite shore. I sit and I breathe because that's all there is to do.

Behind me, the celebration comes alive. The music of the reception pours outside. Rises then falls. And there is a loud drum roll. And I know that people are gathered in a circle around a man and a woman. A boy and a girl. Two people put in the middle, playing their parts in the big show. He's kneeling down. She's pulled up her dress. His hands slide the garter up and up. And up. The crowd laughs and roars with each little inch, everyone connected, existing in the same moment of time.

Except the goose and me.

yellow

✿

Grandma is yellow. Originally diagnosed as jaundice, her subsequent dizzy spells, fatigue and disorientation led to further testing which yielded this - Grandma is dying of liver cancer. She is yellow and has a few weeks to live.

I live six hundred miles away so I call her.

"Grandma, it's me, Aden."

In her polish accent, "I *know* who it is."

I can hear polka music and Grandpa pounding his cane on the floor. He's shouting, *Who is it, Lucy? Who is it?*

"Goddammit, Chester! Shut your mouth! I'm talking to our Grandson!"

Which one? Grandpa chimes.

"The only one that calls, you old fool! Aden!"

"Did I call at a bad time?" I ask.

"No! No! This old fart's driving me crazy! Every time the phone rings he thinks it's a doctor with a miracle cure. That there was some mistake at the clinic. Can't he see? I'm yellow! I'm tired! I just want to sleep, and he's in that kitchen bitching and banging his cane on the floor. Tap! Tap! Tap! Boom! Boom! Boom! The way he carries on I can't even watch golf on TV! I swear to God, I'm going to shove that cane up his ass before it's all over!"

I can see her holding the phone against her big beautiful face. Silver hair. Small thin lips. Big green eyes staring at Grandpa. I cannot for the life of me picture her as yellow.

I ask her, "How are you doing?"

Then I think of how dumb I am for asking.

She's dying. That's how she's doing.

"I'm not dead yet," she says.

"That's good, hey?"

"I guess so..."

She covers the phone, but I can still hear her. She's yelling at Grandpa.

"Turn down that radio and stop banging that cane or I'm going to beat you with it!"

Grandpa hasn't been handling it well. I learned this from my Mom. In fact, everything I know about Grandma's sickness has come from Mom. She's having a tough time too, but she's dealing with it. What's keeping Mom sane while watching her mother die is making the funeral arrangements. She says it's like planning a vacation for someone that'll never return.

Grandma comes back to me. The music is quieter. Grandpa's not banging his cane.

"There," she says. "Finally, some peace and quiet."

"What did you do to him, Grandma?"

"Your Uncle Denny came and got him. They're going to Posen to get some petunias. All I want is to sit on the porch in the summer sun and look at the flowers and birds."

"That'll be nice. You always have the best flowers."

There's a long pause. She breathes deeply. Yawns. As always, it's contagious and I'm yawning too.

"So, what do you want?" she asks.

Her directness is expected. Familiar. But it flusters me all the same.

"I called because I was thinking of coming to visit."

"Visit? Don't be crazy! That's too long to drive!"

"But I want to see you before..."

I cannot finish the sentence.

I listen to the polka music in the background. Hear her breathe. Deep again. Another yawn.

She's in her chair, I bet. In her burgundy recliner that never reclines. The TV is on. Shaky picture detailing the latest golf tournament. Always, she roots for Tiger Woods.

"He's so damned cute!" she's said, time and time again.

In between sips of Milwaukee's Best, *"Look at him. He sure can hit that ball. And the way he moves! It's so graceful!"*

The family thought maybe something was wrong with her a year ago when she took to watching golf so much. And Tiger Woods? A young black man? As far as we knew, Grandma had never even been out of Northern Michigan, let alone seen a black person. But this change, her new interest, was a nice break from the incessant dinging and buzzing of game shows and the greed-driven, sex-filled soap operas that had previously greeted us during our visits. It was really something seeing her there. In her chair. Leaning forward. Smiling. Hands wringing around a can of beer as Tiger stepped up to the tee.

I hear her clearing her throat over the long distance line. Then I hear her taking a drink of something. I look at my watch. It's 11 o'clock in the morning over there in her little white trailer near the lake. About the time she usually cracks her first beer of the day.

"You drinking a beer?"

"Shit no! That damned woman's got me so doped up I can't drink anything but water!"

"What woman?"

"That one from Hospice. She's a pretty little thing. And nice too. If you come home I'll introduce you."

I smile. My Grandma, sick and yellow, but trying to set me up with the woman who has come to help her die.

"She's pretty?" I ask.

"Oh yes! Dark brown hair, brown eyes, *very* pretty. Pretty like that snotty one you used to date."

"You mean Tyler?"

"Yes! That talker! Christ, I'm glad you got rid of her."

"What's this nurse's name? Maybe I know her."

"Oh, you would have to ask...I can't remember her damned name now. Let me ask Grandpa..."

She covers the phone and calls for him. I cringe.

"Chester! What's that nurse's name? Chester!"

She keeps yelling even though Grandpa and Uncle Denny are on the way to Posen for petunias.

✡

Mom says that since Grandma's started dying there's been more action around the trailer than ever before. Aunts cooking meals and cleaning. Uncles planting flowers and trees. Grandchildren stopping by. I can't help thinking how sad and beautiful it is the way death awakens the love in us all.

"Oh shit," Grandma says, "I forgot. He's gone to Posen for potatoes."

"Petunias," I say. "Wasn't it petunias?"

It's cruel the way the mind goes.

I remember a party one summer when the generations had gathered for a reunion and Grandma was the link that brought us together. Grandma was young. Thin and tall. Her skin tight and fresh. She smelled like spearmint. Her mother, my great-grandmother, was there in her wheelchair. Legless and blind. Telling stories the only way she knew how - in Polish. So Grandma sat next to her, holding her purple spotted hands, and she translated the stories for all of us to hear.

"Potatoes. Petunias. It's like my brain's in pea soup."

"It's okay, Grandma."

"No. It's not," she answers. "I'll find out that girl's name when she gets here."

"Do you think it's the medicine they have you on?"

"I'm *old*. That's what it is. I'm falling apart, Aden. I'm falling to pieces and I'm the only one that'll admit it. Everyone else is walking around with blinders on. It's stupid. Here I am, an old woman, and it's like I'm a baby again. People waiting on me hand and foot. Feeding me. Waking me. Putting me to bed. For crying out loud, I'm even wearing diapers again!"

Mom's told me this. That Grandma pees her pants. That Grandma shits her pants. Mom and Uncle Denny clean and change her and put her in her chair on the days she's too weak to do it on her own.

"Well, think of it this way," I say, "You've taken care of everybody and now it's our turn to take care of you."

"It's foolishness! That's what it is. Diapers. Can you imagine?"

I can't imagine it. Like I can't imagine her sitting there all yellow and dying just as the best part of Michigan's summer is coming round. Bright warm days. Cleansing rains. Grass blades and buds greening to life. Grandma is supposed to be stocking bird feeders. Sitting near the kitchen window watching blue jays, sparrows and canaries as they crack and scatter seeds. She's supposed to be doing loads of laundry and hanging wet clothes on the line between the two giant cedar trees so that long waves of color sway in the Long Lake breeze. Instead, Mom goes there every day to change the bedding, to make sure Grandma's taking her medicine, and to make sure she's clean. Mom loads the trunk of her car with dirty clothes, dirty sheets, and cries on the way home because this is not the way it's supposed to be.

"You sure you don't want me to come visit?" I ask.

"What good would it do?"

"Grandma, I want to see you before..."

"I know," she says. "But I don't want you to see me like this."

102

✿

Last time I saw her it was Easter. Her trailer was decked out with stuffed bunnies, plastic eggs, and baskets overflowing with mounds of candy-filled Easter grass. She was sitting in her recliner wearing a white sweatshirt that said, WORLD'S GREATEST GRANDMA! in big red letters. Mom had purchased the thing at K-mart and given it to Grandma for Grandmother's Day on my behalf. Seeing her in it, knowing that she believed it was a gift from me, filled my stomach with shame.

"Wanna beer?" she asked, as I sat down in the only other chair in the room, a plastic lawn chair.

The television was on. Tiger Woods was nine under par. Grandma was glowing as she handed me a beer.

We drank and watched the game. Green grass. Yellow flags. Men in sunglasses, hats, and wrinkle-free clothes. Brand names on everything.

"What do you think about all that advertising?" I asked.

"Who cares?"she said, "It's about men putting their balls in holes!"

We laughed so hard we spilled our beer.

Grandma is not politically correct and she is not always right.

What she *is* is True.

"Life's too short for bullshit!"she said to me after meeting Tyler, the girl I thought I loved. An attractive, one dimensional, vegetarian feminist who believed that it was not only ghastly in this day and age that Grandma raised and butchered chickens, hogs, and rabbits, but that it was heartless and cruel that Grandma believed that it was okay to shoot an

103

animal if it was suffering (in this case, a 13 year-old blind, arthritic hound that she asked Uncle Denny to shoot while we were visiting).

Grandma drank beer and listened to Tyler go on about animal rights, medicare, and the ills of red meat. But when she started in on the harmful effects of alcohol, how it not only destroys the human body, but that its consumption is usually an indication of "*deeper emotional problems*," Grandma looked at me and said, "Talk! Talk! Talk! She talks too much about too many things that don't mean shit!"

Then she looked at Tyler.

"Do you believe in Santa Claus?"

Tyler looked at me uncomfortably. Shifted in her chair and looked up at the fly paper hanging from the ceiling. One fly, still alive, was buzzing furiously. I could tell that she wanted to reach up and let it go.

"I said, DO YOU BELIEVE IN SANTA CLAUS?"

"No. I mean, I used to. When I was a kid, but not anymore."

Grandma sipped her beer.

"Why not?"

"Because, I think Santa is an early form of social control."

Grandma leaned forward and smiled. Her little lips never parted, but stretched wide and made tiny dimples in her big red cheeks.

"Go on," she said.

"I always wanted to wait up and see him, but my mother and father always insisted that I go to bed. They said that if I didn't go to bed Santa wouldn't come. They said that if I wasn't a good little girl I wouldn't get any presents, and that if I didn't do as I was told I would not grow up to be a big girl. But they were wrong. I waited up for him every year, and every year I saw the same thing. My drunk Mom and Dad putting presents under the tree."

"Well then," Grandma interrupted. "They were wrong about one thing."

"Wrong about what?" Tyler asked.

"Look at you now. All grown up into such a big *girl*."

By this time the fly was screaming. Grandma leaned back and looked out the window at a sparrow that was on the window sill looking in. Uncle Denny walked through the yard with a rifle in his hand.

"I beg your pardon," Tyler said, "I am a grown *woman*, not a *girl*!"

Grandma kept on looking at the sparrow. The sparrow kept on looking at her. I watched Grandma and the bird and I waited for the gunshot.

Grandma, sounding bored and tired said, "I know I don't even have to ask this, but you don't believe in God, do you?"

Grandma was right. Tyler didn't. And up until then Tyler had nearly talked me into believing that God was a hoax, a trick, a crutch, that Jesus and sin were part of a story. A story created to keep all of us in line. Under control.

"Everything is not black and white," Tyler hissed. "There is an indefinite state of gray!"

The gunshot was louder than I had expected and it made me jump in my seat. I knew then, as Tyler stood up stomping, that we would not last.

Grandma remained in her chair and spoke quietly.

"I agree. Everything is not black and white. Everything *is* gray. But you *are* a girl and you'll *always* be a girl until you can start believing in things you can't see."

With that, Tyler ran out the door. I looked out the kitchen window. Three canaries had gathered near the sparrow. Uncle Denny was walking by again, this time with a shovel and a burlap sack.

Grandma stood up.

"Time to feed the birds. They're waiting for me."

"Need any help?"

"No. You better go to your girlfriend. Things are going to be different between you now."

"I know," I said.

Grandma turned and opened the fridge. Pickled pig's feet. Pickled herring. Hand-picked eggs. Chicken breasts thawing for supper. She reached in for a beer.

"She's no good for you. A talker that doesn't listen."

Grandma put her hand on my arm and whispered.

"Girls should listen more than they talk. Everyone should. And girls with big mouths have big holes. This one, she's been around. Probably is still going around. I tell you this so you're careful."

I gave Grandma a hug, a kiss on the cheek, and told her I loved her and that I would see her again soon.

"Yeah, yeah, yeah," she gushed. "Stop with the lovey-dovey horseshit! I got to get out there and feed the birds!"

✿

Grandma's banging pots and pans.

"Making lunch, Grandma?"

"Yeah, yeah, yeah. Better get ready to feed the old bastard when he gets back from Posen. If lunch isn't ready, he sits like a canary chirping on the windowsill. *Cheep! Cheep! Cheep! Feed me! Feed me!*"

My yellow Grandma and her yellow birds.

"You don't worry about me, and don't worry about making the trip. You'll see me soon enough."

"Okay, Grandma. But before I go I want you to know..."

I hear her breathing. The slight movement of the phone against her face. The polka music still there, but only slightly, like a whisper. I want to sit and talk until the phone line goes dead. I want to turn up the music and listen as she translates the words. But I can't because it is time to go.

"I know," Grandma says, "I know."

flag day

✿

In a stinking bar - ashtrays and cigarettes, hands holding dirty glasses, puddles of beer on the floor and on the table, the jukebox pounding the stale sweaty air - but I can smell her. Just showered, Ivory skin. Clean, strawberry smelling hair. Our elbows touching and energy shooting from pore to pore, rifling through our layers, pushing deep inside to places that feel familiar because it feels like they've never been touched before.

We sit with co-workers at four long tables that have been joined together to celebrate. Ricky is leaving. The six foot six, hunk of business man who makes more than most of us combined, is leaving us to be an executive for Ford Motor Company in Battle Creek. All I know about Battle Creek is that they make cereal there.

The people surrounding the table are misfits like me. College graduates who work because we need to so that we can do what we love. At the table I'm at there's a guitar player, an artist, and the sculptor, Eileen. She, like the rest of us, has been working at Cheney's Design Inc. for a year and a half because that's how long the company's been around. We came aboard because of promises. Two weeks of vacation, 401k, a casual dress code, and the possibility of stock options.

Ricky had said that coming in on the ground floor of a new company meant one thing - that all of us would be moving up. So far, he's the only one to go, and he's been running the company. I wonder about the loyalty and dedication that Ricky spoke of when he recruited us, and even though I think he's a heartless asshole, I'm sad to see he's leaving because we need people like him to run companies while the rest of us are running the world.

I can't believe how good Eileen smells in all of this. Her scent grounds me and as our legs find each other under the table, I keep fighting myself. She's married, I think. Married and has a kid. I can't decide what it is about her that gets me, but something does. It isn't her body, I think, because frankly she's bigger than any other girl I've ever liked. So maybe it's her long, blonde hair and the way her bangs curl and sweep down in front of her eyes. She looks at me a lot through that wispy hair and she knows that her blue eyes are an advantage. If she works at it, like she usually does, we'll end up calling a cab and heading to my apartment. From there, she'll call her husband. *I'm staying in the city tonight*, she'll say. *Because I'm too drunk to drive. Make sure you get up early enough to get Billy off to school.*

I'll watch her talk and lie and I'll wonder at the foolishness of trust, the boundaries of vows and commitment, but I soon forget them because those are things that do not belong to me. And when the phone's back in its cradle, we'll go right to it. We'll be up and down and all around the apartment, from room to room, chair to floor, carpet to linoleum. When it's all over I'll feel like shit because I can't feel as good as I want to knowing that everything we've just done might be solidifying two advanced tickets to hell. Everything goes away in the darkness though, when she snuggles up and drapes her arms around me, when I feel her breathing.

I'm talking to Chuck, the guitar player, about Hemingway and fishing when Eileen puts her head on my shoulder.

I say to her, like I always do, "People are going to start talking, you know." And she whispers in my ear, "I don't care."

"You guys aren't hiding anything," Chuck says. "It's obvious you two have been fucking for a while now."

The free beer, courtesy of the cigar-puffing, suit-wearing, Ricky, is starting to kick in. Some have heard what Chuck's said, but thankfully Ricky's busy running his mouth about the Mercedes he's going to buy so not everyone has heard.

I lean over the table, but I don't whisper.

"Jesus Christ. You want to get us fired?"

The artist, Jennifer, has two cents to put in.

"Fired for what? For taking some pleasure in this miserable fucking world? This goddamned company...they ought to give everyone a fucking sex slave as a bonus. Wasn't that in our contract?"

We laugh and drink and pour more beer. I see a light come on in the apartment across the street. There's a woman pacing back and forth in front of the window talking on a telephone. She's wearing a white robe and has a towel on her head. The woman has a nice, dark tan, or she might be Mexican. I think about the word Mexican and I wonder if there's a word that's more politically correct. It's hard to tell with all the rightness in the world. All I know for sure is that she's very attractive from what I can see of her. I look for a wedding ring shining through the window glass, or for photographs of children on the wall.

"Hemingway could kick Ricky's ass," Chuck says.

Chuck's an African American, but he's told me it's okay to call him black even though he's a brown chubby man. He's been playing guitar since he was eight years old. He's attended Interlochen, made and sold his own CDs, and plays on Saturdays at the Music Café down the street.

"Ricky's pretty big..." I say, but Jennifer jumps in.

"Before you two start talking about Hemingway and all the asses he could kick, I have something that I've been wanting to ask you, Chuck."

"Sure, go ahead."

"It's of a personal nature."

"Nothing's personal anymore. You know that."

"Okay then. My question is this...In this world of so-called equality, I still think that the reason I haven't made it yet is because I'm a woman. Do you think that the reason you haven't made it yet is because you're an African American?"

"Because I'm black? That's bullshit. I'm making it now. And so are you. To hell with all that. What is making it? Is being like Ricky making it? Because if so, I don't want any part of it. Look at him...what an asshole. Not only could Hemingway kick his ass, I think he would do it for fun."

Miraculously, there's a moment of silence in the bar. The jukebox is changing songs, conversation has lulled, and Ricky's heard what Chuck has said about Hemingway kicking his ass.

"You talking about that fucking writer?"

"You can read, Ricky?" Jennifer yells. Everyone laughs.

"Fuck all of you. I could kick any writer's ass."

"Not Hemingway," I say, and there's more laughter.

Ricky stands up and smiles.

"That's right. You're a writer, aren't you?"

I nod my head and sip my beer. I see that the woman from the lighted apartment is gone. I think maybe she's getting dressed to go out. And I think that it's too bad her bedroom window isn't facing the bar because it would really drum up business. I feel Eileen's hand on my arm. I can tell she doesn't want me to start anything with Ricky because she knows that I won't back down.

My silence and the laughter of others have hurt Ricky. He's getting red in the face and I notice that his big hands are clenched into fists.

"Don't worry about it, Ricky. Hemingway's dead."

"Because someone like me probably kicked his ass."

"Actually, it was something like that."

Across the street, the woman is in her window. She's on the phone again, wearing a black bra and unraveling the towel from around her head. She's bent over to let it all out and for a second I lose sight of her. When she pops up again, I feel warm. From the beer, from Ricky's bullshit, and from the sight of her with that long, dark hair.

"A toast!" Chuck shouts, "To Ricky and to Flag Day!"

"Flag Day?" Ricky says, "Fuck that! To Ricky! And it's no wonder I'm leaving after working with a bunch of freaks and queers for so long. You fuckers really weird me out the way you talk about queer shit all the time. Maybe you are all queer, but it doesn't matter. Let the queers sing their songs, write their stories, and play with clay. In a month I'll be driving by in my new Mercedes, and if you're lucky I'll slow down long enough to wave!"

Everyone laughs and drinks. I turn and look at Chuck.

"Is it really Flag Day?"

"That's what my calendar told me this morning."

Chuck looks over at Ricky. Shakes his head.

"I thought it would be a good idea to try and change the subject. Ricky's pretty loaded."

"Yeah, but Hemingway could still kick his ass."

Eileen pushes her body against mine.

"We ought to go soon," she says.

"What do you mean? The beer's on Ricky and we're just getting started."

"I know, but I'm tired."

I think about the woman in her lighted apartment, slipping a white blouse over her black bra. I imagine she's probably in the bathroom, finishing up her hair, spreading on scented body lotion for someone to inhale.

"Can we hang just a little while longer? I like talking about this shit."

"What shit?"

"Hemingway and stuff."

She rolls her eyes and smiles.

"You boys and your talk. Hemingway's dead and his time is up. He's out and Nicholas Sparks is in. But I don't want to get into this. Maybe Ricky's right. Maybe you boys are a little queer. Do you really like each other?"

"We love each other!" Chuck shouts, as he raises his glass.

All of us clink glasses, except Eileen. She gets up and goes to the bathroom. I imagine that when she gets back it'll be time to go.

"You two *are* fucking, aren't you?" Jennifer asks.

"Leave him alone," Chuck says.

"Why should I?"

"Because you're just jealous that he's the one giving her cock and not you."

"I don't like cock, remember?"

We forget sometimes that Jennifer is a lesbian because she is amazingly beautiful. She is a tall, shapely, red head. Besides being an artist, she's a lifeguard and she runs in marathons. The woman is a glorious physical specimen.

"That's what I mean. You want to be the one giving it to her."

Chuck smiles. Jennifer pauses to sip her drink, and I can tell she's thinking of something to say. It's a nice break in the action because I like the way her lips touch the glass.

"Very funny, Charlie, but I'm afraid she's not worthy of my cock."

"You mean the plastic one in your dresser drawer?"

Chuck laughs and so do I because all of us are getting drunk and I'm thinking that if Hemingway was alive I bet he wouldn't mind being right here with us. Drinking, laughing, and talking shit - especially on Flag Day.

Ricky's drinking shots. There's a busty waitress making him keep his hands off her and the glass. He's told he has to keep his head tilted back and remain still so that she can pour the shot down his throat. Ricky tells her that he'll sit still if she pours the drink from her tits. He says that there's a big tip in it for her, so the girl straddles him, puts the shot glass between her tits and pours it down his throat beautifully. It doesn't look like it could be done better in a movie.

The shot, however, is too much for him. He gags and coughs and cusses out the waitress as he stuffs a five-dollar bill deep into her cleavage. He puts his hand over his mouth and heads toward the bathroom.

"I hope he pukes his guts out," Jennifer says.

"Do you think Hemingway puked?" Chuck asks.

"Sure, that's how you build stamina, isn't it?"

"You two shouldn't idolize Hemingway so much," Jennifer says.

"Sure we should. We're in our twenties. Isn't that right, Chuck?"

"In our time that's what we need. We need another Hemingway."

I fill all of our glasses, including Eileen's, and I hope that when she's done in the bathroom she'll want to sit and drink some more. I glance at the apartment window across the street and the light is off.

The woman is gone.

"I don't know why we talk about him like we do," I say. "I like his writing because it's brutal and honest. It's about natural things."

"I think you boys love him because he's a symbol of masculinity and because it makes you feel tough. I mean, do you really think he could survive in our world today?"

"No, he isn't a symbol and he couldn't live in our time. We don't give a shit about anything but making money, buying things, and creating walls to call home. We're a bunch of soulless assholes. Look at us. The only reason we're here is to drink for free. We sit and bitch about the weight of a politically correct world. And all I really want to do is get drunk, go home, fuck and fall asleep."

"That's good to know," Eileen says, as she comes up from behind and puts her arms around me.

Jennifer drains her beer then gets up to leave.

"Okay kids. The shit's getting deep, so I think I'll be going. I'm supposed to go running tomorrow morning."

Chuck stands and stretches.

"Yeah, I better get moving too. I have to be at the Café early tomorrow to set up. You guys coming down to listen?"

We tell him that we'll be there because we will. We have to stick together in all of this because there aren't many of us left. If there are, they're silent and living alone in apartments across the street from bars. They're coming home late from work, dressing up, putting on something new, so that they can go out and dance, and drink, and look for something that's missing so that they'll have meaning.

Eileen sits next to me.

"Maybe I should go home tonight. You know?"

I wonder what's happened in the bathroom to change her mind. If it is Flag Day and the fourteenth of June, I know her period's about two weeks away. So it must be something else. Guilt, perhaps. Or maybe she just wants to go home. To make that long drive in the dark night. Alone.

To their house on the hill. Where she will undress. Get into bed. And hold him. So that he will smell it. The beer. The smoke. An unknown scent. And finally, she will have shown him her infidelity.

Outside the window, the woman from the apartment is walking across the street. Under the lights, in her white blouse and black skirt, she's looking like some Dark Lady Shakespeare would write about. When she reaches our side of the street, a man on a bicycle nearly plows into her. He has a long, scraggly beard and is wearing a backpack against his naked back. Sticking out of the pack, wavering through the night air is an American Flag. The woman is shocked and scared, and in an instant dictated by nothing but invisible fate, our eyes meet through the window glass. I can see she's rethinking everything.

"Yeah, maybe sleeping alone will be good," I say to Eileen as I take another drink.

I hear the door open and some of the bar goes out into the night. I wonder if the shirtless man with the flag has heard anything. I wonder if anyone else along the street outside is awake. If they are, what are they doing? Are they drinking? Watching television? Surfing the Internet? Does anyone read anymore?

Eileen eyes the Dark Lady as she walks into the bar then looks back at me.

"I could stay a little while longer," she says.

"No, that's all right. I want to get out of here before Ricky gets back from the bathroom anyway. I don't even want to say goodbye to that sonofabitch."

All of us walk out together, through smoke, music and laughter. I watch the Dark Lady take a stool at the bar and by the way she moves and sits I can tell she's someplace familiar. I catch sight of Ricky coming out of the darkness. He's wiping his mouth. He's making his way to the bar. I know that once I'm outside, if I turn around, he'll be at her side promising to buy the next round.

the black

✿

We've set up camp. Stretched tarps from red elm to red elm to cover our site, chopped plenty of wood for the fire, and put up the tent. We've made it through one day and one night of poor weather. Made it through by playing euchre, eating baked beans and venison jerky, and by drinking. Made it through in familiar brotherly silence. Communicating through proximity. Nods, hand gestures, facial expressions. I'm relieved that we don't have to talk to be speaking.

It's early May. An overcast day. Cold and peppered with sprinkles. Waders on, ultra-light rods and reels, 4lb test. Light tackle. Tiny spinners and small jigs. Soft-bodied, plastic grubs and worms with curly tails. Plastic frogs and artificial minnows with yellow eyes. Tiny hooks shoved into pieces of nightcrawler or salmon eggs.

We're in it. Thigh deep in the icy water of the Black River. Wading and casting. Wading and casting some more.

"She didn't love you, anyway," Seth says, taking off one lure and putting on another.

I cast. The current moves the crawler downstream, parallel to the bank for several yards, then pulls the line away, into a dark spot in the water.

"I know she didn't."

"Why'd you stay with her?" he asks.

It feels like I have a bite. I want to believe I do, but when I give the line a jerk, I'm snagged.

"I stayed with her because that's what we're supposed to do."

Seth casts upstream. Reels with the current.

"She cheated on you, you know."

I pull on my line. Try not to break it, but try to get free. There's give in whatever I've hooked. I pull. It moves. But it will not let go.

It has been six months since Kali and I have parted. I only miss her sometimes. Like now, when fishing such a pretty place with my brother. When life is starting to come around in Northern Michigan. Greening grass. Yellowing flowers. Buds on trees. Birds in song on limbs and in flight. Muskrats on the shoreline and swimming the stream, mouths filled with grasses and sticks. Trout darting out from under hollows in the bank, disappearing up or down the stream.

"I know she cheated," I say.

Seth sees I'm snagged. He casts and reels, and waits. There's a dark place ahead of us. Where the stream bends around between two high, sandy banks. There are red pines broken down and submerged in the water. A wide channel has hollowed the bank and runs deep under the fallen trees. It's got the makings of a good hole.

"Why don't you break it?" he asks.

I know I could. The light line breaks easily. It is only a hook and a crawler. But letting it snap, giving up and letting go, feels wrong.

"You go on," I say. "There'll be brookies there."

Seth moves ahead. Barely makes ripples. Is soundless in the rushing and gurgling of the stream. He is a lean silhouette in the shadow of the tall banks. A body and mind like mine. Of the same blood. But I know he knows more about everything. He ties the right knots. Identifies the trees. Knows a bird by its song. Seth has never loved a woman in this world, but he knows my marriage has failed. And he knows why. He knows Kali, of her infidelity, but he also knows of mine. How I've cheated myself by living a lie.

I wade toward the place where my line meets the water. I reel to keep the line taught, but whatever I've snagged is giving way.

"Fish on!" Seth shouts. His voice rises from the stream and rings between the tall, sandy banks so loud and strong that I'm sure they will crumble down and bury us.

I glance over. He's leaned back slightly. Rod tip high. Reeling with fury.

I've reached the place where my line is snagged. I bend over to block the sky's reflection so that I can see. And at my feet, against a bottom of sand, smooth rock and pebble, is a dead deer. My bronze hook is caught in a bright white rib. Alongside other hooks and lures and broken line. The hair that's left is black and shaggy, like a dirty old rug. Bits of hide cling to the skull. The legs are stripped to the bone. It is a doe. And she has drown. Or fallen through winter's ice. Or been shot and left behind. To rot underwater.

Seth is netting his first fish. Holding it up for me to see. Smiling like there's nothing better, as if things could never be better, so I reach down into the icy water and free my line. I move toward him casting and reeling. Wading as slowly and carefully as I can.

winter

✿

My wife is on the telephone. Talking with her lover. So I stand outside. Fingers aching cold. Eyes watering at the sky. It's too late in the year, but there's a V of geese flying above me. Struggling to keep formation. So low, I can hear the whistling of wings. They are headed south. Or maybe not even that far. Perhaps the city, only thirty miles away, will be warm enough. Year-round parks. Bird feeders and hand-outs. Ponds that don't freeze. The birds honk as they ascend into thick, gray clouds that layer and fold. Create shapes and forms. A heart. A horse. A ring. The face of Jesus in the sky.

Finally, filled up with cold, I go inside.

I stomp the snow off my boots. Plates and cups rattle on shelves behind cupboard doors.

"Why are you stomping? You know I'm on the phone!"

She says this with her hand clamped over the mouthpiece. To stifle our sound. As if any of this can be kept silent.

I stomp more, then move to the coffee pot. Her cup is there. Lipstick on the rim. I touch it then look at the color on my fingertip. It is not quite red, and it is something new.

I pour coffee. Add milk and sugar. I stir. Clanking the spoon inside the cup. She's twirling her hair with fury. Glaring at me, as she listens to her lover. They are making plans. I know this because she has told me so. In all of this she has told me plenty. She has been honest. She's told me the Truth.

Finally, she says, she's fallen in love. Our marriage was something else. Not love, but something to help us find Love. She has found hers. I will find mine. Our divorce is necessary, she says. It is a parting of ways that will free us. And we need to be free because we are no longer the people we used to be.

I look at the paintings that hang on the kitchen wall. There is one of us. It is springtime and we are newlyweds. A moment fixed in watercolor. We are smiling and holding hands. Next to that is another painting. Of Jesus. In oils. Leaning forward under the weight of the cross he carries. Sin and hope. Promise and regret. Our sacrificial lamb.

"I can't wait to see you," my wife tells the other man. "I'm taking care of things on this end and I'll be leaving shortly."

I have not seen my wife in weeks. She has come now to deliver paperwork. To resolve our broken life with a folder of documents. A list.

"I don't want this to be messy," she says to me, as she returns the receiver to its cradle.

"It's already messy," I say.

She takes a sheet of paper from the folder she's brought. Holds it out for me to take.

"Here's a list. Things I want to keep. Things you can have. I trust we know enough of each other that we don't need the lawyers to make these decisions."

The list is written on personalized stationery. Kali Beck, it says. Already, she's dropped my last name.

"I'll look it over later," I say, and I squeeze my coffee cup.

She sighs. Fills her cup over the sink Like she's always done. As usual, she only pours half a cup and she spills a little.

I stare out the window into the field across the road. There are turkeys marching through dead grass. I count twenty-seven hens. There isn't a tom in sight. The turkeys gather near a row of abandoned hay bales. They peck and scratch the ground.

"Aren't you going to say anything?" she asks, sipping her coffee.

I raise my cup to my lips as slowly as I can. Take a long, noisy sip.

"I know when it happened," I say.

"What?"

"When it ended."

She sets her cup down. Leans against the counter top. Stares into the floor.

"Listen, I don't want to fight. I just came to give you the papers and say goodbye."

I feel something shaking loose inside. I hold my cup tighter. Move closer to her.

"One night, I came home early and you were in the shower. The phone rang. I answered it, and I could *feel* him on the line."

She turns and reaches for her coat.

"He didn't say anything, but I knew he was there. It was like both of us were standing silent, face to face in the dark. And I wanted him to say something, to ask for you, but he didn't. And I walked to the bathroom door with the phone in my hand, and I wanted to confront you. Both of you. But he'd hung up before I could do anything. So I stood there, outside the bathroom, waiting for you, not knowing what to do, trying to put together the pieces. And then, that's when I heard it."

Kali slips her arms through her sleeves. Pulls on her hat.

"Heard what?"

"The shower spraying. Water drops against the shower curtain. And you, my wife. Singing a song I'd never heard before. That's when I knew."

She looks into my eyes and I feel it, as I've always felt it, but I see that she feels nothing. Her brown eyes are glass. Small, dark surfaces for reflecting the world.

"Stop it," she says.

"After I heard you singing, I walked outside and stood in the dark looking at our house. I thought about all of things we had shared. And all of the things we had planned. I stared for a long time at the bathroom window. Through the shades and the steam, I could see a shadow. An outline of a woman. But it wasn't you."

"It *was* me," Kali says. "It was me, but..."

She moves away. Toward the paintings that hang on the kitchen wall.

"I forgot about this," she says. And she stands before Jesus. Reaches up. Touches him

"I didn't put this on the list."

"But you made it."

"I know I did. But you can keep it."

Kali turns. Faces me. Our eyes lock. I feel it again, as I've felt it thousands of times, but she shows nothing.

I turn away. Look out the kitchen window. Big flakes drift and whirl. The turkeys are gone. The sky is white. And behind me, Kali opens the door. There is a moment of shared silence. Like two strangers passing in the dark. And then, she is gone.

after the rain

☼

He comes to me. Big, brown eyes. Smiling.

"Daddy, let's pick night crawlers."

"What for?"

He does a little jump. Claps his hands.

"For fishing!"

My boy. Five years old. Tickled with the notion of traipsing through puddles, picking slimy worms.

"But we can't go fishing today," I say. "Mom will be here soon."

Undefeated. Still brimming with smile. Another jump. More clapping hands.

"We can go next weekend!" he cheers.

"Okay, buddy. Let's get something to put them in."

It doesn't take long. He runs to the kitchen sink, reaches way up high and takes a cereal bowl from atop the stack of dirty dishes.

"We'll use this!"

He grabs his baseball cap from the table and runs out the door. Barefoot.

Dark is coming on and I know Anna is already on her way. She'll arrive shortly. In her boyfriend's car. A sleek, sporty deal that's always shined up and spotless. Today, I'm sure she's dreading the drive down my muddy dead-end road.

She'll be here within minutes. I know this because it is Sunday. And she always comes early on sundays. It's so they can go for ice cream.

A little family tradition that we had together, but that they now have on their own.

I walk barefoot through the wet grass. Searching the yard. Under rocks. Near the sidewalk. But there aren't any worms anywhere. When I get to the flower garden, the one Anna had labored over every spring and summer, I stop.

Two sunflowers have found a way through the tangled weeds. Their big, colorful heads droop. Water drips from the yellow petals. Slips off the leaves.

Kneeling in the driveway. Cereal bowl in one hand. The other fishing around in a puddle. My boy pulls worms from the water. Holds them up to the sky. Lets them stretch out. Looks at each one as if it's the first he's ever seen.

"This is a big one!" he says, putting it in the bowl, running toward me.

And it *is* a big one. Twice as fat and twice as long as any of the others he has. In all, I count five.

"How many have you got in there?" I ask, crouching down.

He sets the bowl on the ground. Takes them out one by one. They twist and writhe in the gravel and sand until they are so full of dirt they can't move. My son picks up each one, brushes it off and counts as he places them back into the bowl.

"Five!" He beams. "One. Two. Three. Four. Five!"

"You sure can count well."

"Dan has me count everything," he says.

132

My heart plummets. But I smile. Tussle his hair. Pull him near. He smells as beautiful as he did the first day I held him. Five years ago. Like yesterday. Sitting on the edge of the hospital bed. Looking at his little pink face. Anna's hand on my back. Her head on my shoulder.

Dan is the new man in my son's life. He wakes early. Makes pancakes and smoky links. Squeezes oranges for fresh juice. On the way out the door to his six-figure career, he kisses Anna's cheek. Gives my boy a big hug.

"That's good," I say. "Count all you can."

It's all I can muster.

Thunder booms. He looks into the sky. Smiles wide.

"No lightning?" he asks.

I want to look up, to watch for the burst of light in the dark sky, but I can't because I hear Anna coming. She has turned onto my road. Is taking it slow. Making sure to avoid puddles and soft spots.

"You can't always see it," I say.

"What?" he asks.

"The lightning. You can't always see it."

We stand up. Anna pulls into the driveway. She looks radiant. Better than I ever remember. She smiles at him. Toots the horn. Waves.

He is all smiles. Waving back. Jumping. Clapping those little hands.

"Ice cream!" he yells. "Ice cream!"

I pick him up and hold him toward the sky. Swing him in big circles. He giggles. And it's the best sound in the world.

"Come with us, Dad!"

I stop the circles. Bring him down. And I hold him. Breathe in as much of him as I can. Because I know that these days will not last.

"Maybe another time, buddy."

He wraps his arms around my neck. Kisses my cheek.

I let him go. Onto his little bare feet. He runs away into the house.

There is a short moment while he's gone and it's just me and Anna again. Our eyes meet in the raindrops. Through the car's tinted glass. She gives me a little smile. Flashes the headlights two times. Our little sign. Hello and goodbye.

He runs out of the house. Still barefoot. Carrying his shoes in hand.

"Bye Dad!" he shouts, "Love you!"

I wave. Watch him get in and kiss his Mom on the cheek. She hugs him. Kisses his forehead. He buckles up. They back out of the driveway. Pull onto the road. And then, they are gone.

Above me, the sky lets loose. Lightning flashes. Raindrops fall. And I stand in the driveway. Holding the bowl of worms. Counting the seconds until thunder booms.

holiday cheer

✿

I visit him because he's a crazy fucker and he needs me. If I don't go there, he'll louse up big time. And that will be that. He'll make toast in the bathtub. Jump off the roof. Hang himself with Christmas lights. Which would be fitting, since it *is* Christmas and all.

He's not answering his phone. It rings and rings and rings. This isn't a surprise. He doesn't always answer it. Not right away. He lets it ring, watches it ring, and if the ring sounds different from what he thinks it should, he answers it. It's hit or miss with this guy. More often than not, I'm a hit, but today it's Christmas Day, the only day when I actually plan on seeing the damned loony, and I'm a miss.

Or he is.

I'm not sure.

What I am sure of is that I have twelve miles to drive through a snowstorm to spread some holiday cheer, and he's got me worried.

He says awful things sometimes. Like earlier today, when the crazy ass *did* answer the phone and I had to hang up on him. I couldn't help it. I had to. He said that all he wanted for Christmas was a gun. He sang that damned song, the one that goes "*All I want for Christmas is my two front teeth, my two front teeth*" but he changed the words to "*All I want for Christmas is a real big gun, a real big gun.*" He kept singing it and singing it, over and over, so I hung up the phone. I had to. It was pretty scary. Really.

And now I'm calling him back, and he won't answer the phone. Not even on Christmas. So, I load up what I got for him. Six-foot-tall, fake tree. Two dozen Christmas bulbs. Twenty-five feet of silver garland.

He's already got lights. The day after Thanksgiving he somehow managed to get to a store and buy lights.

Or maybe he stole them. I don't know.

Of course, I got him what he wanted. A gun. It's a toy, but Catchey won't know the difference. He's wrecked. Not all there, if you know what I mean.

It's a lever-action, black steel, Daisy Red Ryder BB gun. Without the BB's. I kept those. The last thing I want him doing is loading the sonofabitch and putting an eye out. Especially mine.

I don't wrap the gun because I know if I do, he'll have a fit. He's got an issue with Christmas wrap. Years ago, his baby brother, Jeffery, choked on a wad of it and died. He was only four. Catchey was eight. When his parents came into the living room, they couldn't tell if Catchey was shoving the wad of paper in, or trying to get it out. That morning, before the Christmas wrap incident, Catchey had threatened to kill his little brother because he had received more toys than he did. So you see, even as a kid, Catchey had issues. A mean streak. Extreme highs and extreme lows. But when a kid's eight years old and his baby brother dies, you give him the benefit of the doubt.

Unfortunately, since that gift of doubt, it's all been downhill.

His parents are dead too.

His dad died in a fire. Fell asleep in his hunting blind because of the fumes from his heater. Was cooked up when his pant leg got too close to the flame. Catchey was sixteen.

Two years later, his mom whacked herself out. Took a bottle of

Tylenol PM and washed it down with a bottle of Absolut. Catchey found her, but didn't report it. Didn't call for help. Didn't do anything. He ordered Chinese food and stayed in his room for days. Watched the Yankees in the World Series. Finally, Yang, from Bin Bin's House of Dong, noticed the stink of the body as he delivered half a dozen crab cheese wontons and a pepper-steak entrée. When Yang returned to the House of Dong, he called the cops.

When they arrived, they knew something was afoot. Catchey had draped a large Yankees' pennant over his mother's body. He had his pants down, was sitting in his own shit, crying on the floor next to her. Both of them surrounded by empty Chinese food cartons.

I pass Bin Bin's House of Dong as I drive through the snow. I get stuck at a stoplight, but some tis-the-season-to-be-jolly Samaritan stops and pushes me out. I keep right on going once he's pushed me out, and I feel sort of bad for not saying thank you, or for giving a friendly wave, but I got my hands on the wheel at ten and two, and I know God will be proud of me for running to see if Catchey's okay. Especially on baby Jesus' birthday.

The push out of the snow was all I needed. An angel. A Samaritan. Somebody looking to make a few bucks. Whatever the case, I get through the snow all right and before I know it, I'm standing at Catchey's door with my arms full of Christmas.

"Merry Christmas, Catchey!"

He doesn't come to the door.

"Open up, Catchey! It's Santee Claus and he's got presents!"

Still no answer.

I stand waiting for as long as I can. I think about turning back. I could decorate my own place. Whip up the tree, wrap it in garland, drink a few beers, put up some lights and then sit in my living room shooting them out with the BB gun. But no, I think. Poor Catchey. That dumb sonofabitch could have his head in the oven, or be lighting himself on fire. Like he's done before.

That was another scary one.

"I'm going to light me on fire!" he'd screamed through the phone line one morning.

"No, Catchey. Don't do it. You'll get in trouble. You'll hurt yourself."

"I'm going to! Come watch! On the corner!"

When I got to the corner outside Catchey's place, he was there all right. Holding a picture of himself with his family. Dousing it with lighter fluid.

"Time to go!" he screamed.

"Catchey, don't burn that picture! It's the only one you got!"

He burned it anyway, or at least part of it. Sparked a match, and held it to the picture until he burned his fingers. When the picture hit the ground, still flaming, Catchey fell on top of it and smothered it with his body.

"I save! I save!" he yelled.

And I guess, in his own way, he did.

The picture, burned to a crisp, hangs on his kitchen wall.

I know I have to go into the apartment. I have to because I'll feel guilty if I don't.

As usual, the door's unlocked.

Inside, Catchey's under the kitchen table with a silver colander on his head. He's flat on the floor with pillows stacked in front of him, aiming a wooden spoon at me as I bend over to look at him.

"Catchey, what are you doing?"

"You're dead! You talk no more! Shut up! You're dead!"

"Catchey, listen. I'm sorry I hung up on you. I'm here to celebrate. It's Christmas!"

By now, Rucks, Catchey's big, fat calico, has appeared from the bathroom. He's rubbing his ass on my leg.

"Rucks get you! Rucks get you!" Catchey yells, as he clangs the spoon against the colander on his head. "Rucks kill bad!"

I make like I'm going to swat the cat and it runs into the bathroom. I set the Christmas goodies on the kitchen table. Catchey reaches up and grabs my leg.

"You Santee?"

I smack Catchey in the noggin. The colander rings like a Christmas bell.

"Get out from under there!"

Catchey lets go of my leg. He scrambles out from under the table and stands next to me. He puts his head on my shoulder, whimpers as tears swell up in his eyes.

I walk away from him and take the tree into the living room. He's got his recliner turned facing the window. Covered in Christmas lights. The television is face down on the floor. There's dried cat puke everywhere.

Catchey sobs in the kitchen. It bothers me because all he wants for Christmas is a gun, and the gun is sitting right there on the kitchen table. All he's got to do is stop crying and open his eyes.

I try not to think about it as I get the tree out of the box. It's in three pieces. The branches all folded up, but it's a breeze to put together, and I'm surprised at how real it looks, even up close. I sniff the needles for the hell of it, and I swear I can smell pine. I pick up the box and read it. It says nothing about being a scented tree.

"Catchey, stop crying! Come smell this tree!"

He doesn't come, but Rucks does. Comes purring alongside me. Rubbing my leg. I kick the little bastard and he slides across the floor into the wall. He stops and wretches and wretches and hacks up a milky gob of hair.

I walk away, into the kitchen, because I need the bulbs and garland to decorate the tree. When I get to the table, I notice that the gun's gone. It's gone and so is Catchey. I listen and can hear him in the bathroom. He cocks and fires, cocks and fires. Squeals with joy.

It almost makes me smile.

I put the garland and the bulbs on the tree and I'm wrapping the final loop of lights around it when Catchey comes into the room holding the gun.

"A gun!" he shouts, delighted like a child.

The moment might be perfect, a real instance of Christmas spirit, but Catchey's naked from the waist down.

He does this all the time.

"Where are your pants?"

"I shit!" he yells, still absolutely tickled that he's holding a gun.

What can I do?

I walk over and plug in the lights. The phony tree looks great.

"Catchey, come smell the tree."

"A gun! A gun! A gun!"

He cocks the gun, points the barrel into my face, and pulls the trigger. A blast of air whops me in the eye.

"I kill!" he shouts, ecstatically, "I kill!"

Rucks is behind Catchey. Front paws on the back of Catchey's legs. Trying to smell his ass.

I turn the recliner around and take a seat. Catchey moves toward the tree. Bends over to put the gun under it, and I can see shit and bits of toilet paper smeared around his crack.

Rucks runs up behind him. Sniffs away.

I stare into the lights.

"I leave the gun for Santee," Catchey whispers. Then he stands up and walks toward me. Stands right in front of me. His cock and balls dangling in my face.

I stand up. Put my hands on his shoulders. And I turn him around.

Poor Catchey. I just want to hug him, to hold the crazy bastard and let him know that things will be okay, but I can't because they probably won't be. He's too far gone, and all I can do is pretend that things have not come to this.

"I give Santee gun," he whispers.

Rucks is at it again. Sniffing and rubbing, so I boot him once more. He slides into the base of the tree, casually rights himself, then lifts his leg and begins licking. When he's satisfied, he stretches out onto his side and paws at something I cannot see. His tail whisks back and forth like a pendulum.

"Catchey, Santee doesn't come to little boys who can't wipe their own asses."

I know I shouldn't say things like that, but it's ridiculous. Nonsense. He's a grown man.

Some days he can get out and walk to the store himself. Some days he can cook for himself. I've seen him come out of the bathroom clean and shaven, fresh and new. And I can't believe him today. Why can't he make it through today without shitting himself?

I make him stand in the tub and I get the water started.

He breathes deeply. Wrings his hands.

"Sit," I say.

He does, and then he rocks back and forth as I fill the tub. I use as much cold water as I can because I'm afraid of what might happen. And then, it does happen. I try not to look, but I do, I always do, and there it is. Catchey's throbbing dick, getting bigger and bigger and bigger. He reaches for it, and I do what any civilized being would do. I pop him in the back of the head. Hard.

I shove a bar of soap into his hands and order him to scrub. He bawls and wails, but I remind myself that sometimes you gotta be tough. Especially with people you love.

I push him over, grab the shower head, and spray his ass as clean as I can.

"Stand up and dry off," I say, as sternly as possible. "When I come back, I want you spic and span!"

As I walk out, I pick up his pants. There's shit all over them, so I put them in the tree box and head outside into the snow, so that I can throw everything away into the dumpster.

How does it happen?

How does any of this happen?

A couple of bad shakes. A stacked deck. A bad deal. Turds in the gene pool.

There are layers of meaning to sift through, but I don't have the time. I don't want the time. I'm afraid of what I might find.

All around me snow, lights, and holiday cheer. Families getting together. Bundled up and driving by. They'll suck down eggnog. Share presents. Make memories. Carve the Christmas beast. All of them living better than Catchey and me.

I throw the shitty Christmas tree box into the dumpster. I look up into the sky toward Catchey's apartment window, expecting to see a burst of flames. A dangling rope. Or Catchey on the edge, getting ready to jump. But from the sidewalk, through huge, whirling snowflakes, all I can see is one thing. Catchey dripping wet and butt-naked, yanking lights off the tree.

<u>in the moonlight</u>

✿

Somehow, I've made it home. And I've come to. In my bed. Fully clothed. On top of the covers. And someone's coming up the stairs. Deliberately trying to be quiet. But the old staircase is creaking and popping. Giving them away. Mapping their ascent to my room.

I try sitting up, but I'm hung-over and still a little drunk, so the ceiling spins and the walls go whirling. I settle my head back into the pillow, and as I'm about to close my eyes, a dark figure enters the room. I try to swallow, to speak, but my mouth's so dry it feels sewn shut. *This could be it*, I think. An intruder. A killer. The shadow of death. My doom. But when the figure meets the moonlight, and she is revealed to me, the spinning stops, and I am comforted.

It is Hannah. My waitress from the bar.

"Are you okay?" she asks, as she hands me an icy glass of water.

I gulp and drink until my eyes are teary and my head aches with cold.

"Better now."

She takes the empty glass. Sets it on the bedside table. Then she stretches out alongside of me. As if we've been doing this for years.

Hannah's my waitress on the weeknights at Sammy's Bar. She brings powerful vodka tonics, and I drink them as I go over the day's work. Pages of writing in need of attention from a much more distant and relaxed editorial eye. We've always been friendly. I'm one of her priority customers, she says. It's because I drink a lot and end up tipping very well.

I take a long, deep breath of her. She smells clean and familiar.

Like my soap and my shampoo.

"I showered. I hope you don't mind."

She snuggles up to me. Puts her hand over my heart.

"Still ticking?" I ask.

"For now," she says, patting her fingers against my chest, keeping time with the beat.

"But if you keep drinking like this it's gonna give out one day."

A big white moth flies up to the window, flutters and beats against the screen. Somewhere, beyond us, coyotes yip and howl. Their sounds grow and rise into high-pitched cries.

"Why do they do that?" she asks.

"The moths or coyotes?"

"Coyotes."

"Maybe they're trailing a deer."

"They sound so sad."

"What's sad is that you had to drive me home."

"I *had* to," she says. "It was partly my fault."

"What was?"

"You drinking so much. I should have cut you off."

"I wouldn't have let you."

"I know. I tried once, but you insisted on more."

"I always want more. That's the way it is with me."

"Still, I should know better. Letting you drink so much could get me fired."

She stops her fingers and quiets her hand.

"Or get you killed."

The coyotes have gone silent. They've caught the deer, or lost the scent, or moved out of earshot.

The moth beats against the screen, convinced it can get inside.

I know I shouldn't do it, but I slide my arm around her, and pull her closer to me.

"It won't kill me, but you might lose your job."

"I might," she answers.

"You don't want to wait tables your whole life anyway, do you?"

It's a rotten thing to say, but I've said it, and now it's out there. Here. Sinking into us. Making up the night.

A bat sails past the window then circles back and snatches the moth from the window screen.

"Waiting tables pays the bills," she says.

"And then some," I add, because I remember her car. Black and sporty. Smooth lines. Fancy wheels. A dashboard full of glowing lights. Stereo. Navigational system. Climate control. A car so immaculate and fresh with new leather scent that even in my drunken stupor I was aware enough to knock the dirt from my shoes before getting in.

She lifts her head and looks at me.

"What's that supposed to mean?"

"Means you must be doing okay. You have a nice car."

"What does a car have to do with anything?"

"It's an all-American measure of success."

She pulls away from me.

"It was a gift."

"From an admirer?"

She sits up. Flings long blonde hair from her face over her shoulder.

"Proud grandparents, I'll have you know. They gave it to me when I got my master's degree."

"Master's degree?"

"Yes. In art history. And it just so happens that a master's degree is *exactly* what a girl needs to wait tables these days."

"Why don't you teach?"

She moves close again. Puts her face into my chest. Breathes a deep breath of me.

"I don't want to," she says, sliding her hand down my chest, to my belly, then to my zipper. She pulls it down very slowly, stops midway.

"Sounds dumb, doesn't it?"

"You love art?" I ask.

She straddles me.

"I *love* painting and taking pictures."

"Then paint and take pictures."

"Could I take pictures of you?"

"What for?"

"For me," she pauses, as if searching for a reason that's more pleasing to me. "And for your book covers. People should know what you look like."

"Why?"

"It will help sales. Readers want to know what their writers look like. I would have bought your books if I'd known what you looked like."

"I don't want sales."

"Then why do you write?"

"Why do you paint?"

Hannah moves her face toward mine.

"But you have such a nice face. Why hide it?"

Gently, I push her away.

"What are you doing?" she asks.

"I have to use the bathroom."

She sighs. Rolls onto her back. Puts her hands behind her head and yawns.

I stand and I wobble, and I make my way through the room. A slanting shadow on the wall. Another dark figure in the moonlight.

"Don't fall down the stairs," she says.

I imagine falling and cracking my head open. Being on my back with the ceiling and walls spinning all around me, hearing Hannah run down the steps. Seeing her over me, watching her fade to black as she reaches to check my pulse.

"Leave me if I do."

"That's awful," she says.

And I walk down the stairs.

The bathroom's all moist air, Ivory soap, and Pantene. The mirror of the medicine cabinet is fogged over. Except for the place she has drawn a smiley face and written *GOOD MORNING*!!

I open the shower curtain and she is everywhere. On the damp towel hanging over the side of the tub. In the foamy bubbles on the shampoo bottle. In the long hairs across the drain. She is the water. Droplets beaded up and glistening, making chrome sparkle and ceramic shine.

I turn away from it then stand at the toilet, pissing, aiming as steadily as I can, looking out the steamy bathroom window at deer that are nibbling away at the garden I've let go. Four mature does. Three fawns from this spring. They're eating breakfast in the moonlight. Working on what drives them. Energy. Sustenance. Survival. But some of them will not make it. Not through deer season. Not through winter. Maybe not even through the rest of the day.

When I turn to leave the bathroom, I notice Hannah's bra and panties hanging from the towel hook on the door. I know I shouldn't, but I touch them anyway. I lift and hold them. Move the cotton fabrics between my fingers, and I imagine them always being there. Always here. Hanging on hooks. Draped over doorknobs. Slung over the backs of chairs. It's something I want so much that I know it's something I cannot have.

I put the bra and panties back where they don't belong. Wipe the smiley face from the mirror. Take one last look outside to see a fawn venturing off on its own. Walking away from the garden through the field with its nose to the ground. Ears up. Tail twitching back and forth. Moving through the ditch and onto the road.

I start upstairs knowing that she's naked. That she's pulled back the covers, and is on top of the sheets. That she's watching night give way to morning, listening for my movement, the noise a body makes when ascending a staircase.

We know what it'll be like. Two strangers coming together. And we know that once the daylight breaks, whatever we've made will be gone because things cannot stay the same once they've been shared in the dark.

dead bunnies

✿

It is seven o'clock. Saturday morning. Elizabeth is beside the bed. Shaking me.

"Daddy, there's another one!"

I open my eyes. Stretch.

"Another what?" I ask.

"Another bunny!"

I sit up. Look at her. She is upset. But not in tears like the other two times.

"Okay, honey. I'll take care of it."

She climbs into bed. Snuggles up next to me.

"Why does he keep doing it?" she asks.

"That's what cats do, honey. They hunt."

I am slightly confused as to how it's come to this. My daughter and I living this new life. Miles away from the city. Drafty old house. Ramshackle church. Renovating. Rebuilding. Adjusting. While Maggie, my wife, rests in a hospital bed. Fed by bagged fluids. Relieved by tubes. Healing in medicated sleep. So that some day soon we can all be together and finish this dream. A big two-story house on ten acres to raise a garden and a family. A small country church turned into an art studio and a library. But for now, we are stuck in the middle. Biding our time.

Elizabeth is struggling, but doing well. And this is a surprise to me. Not because she has been uprooted from home, school, and her friends, but because she was the one that found her. My wife. Her mother. On the day of the move. Naked in the bathroom. Curled up between the toilet and tub. Blood running from a crack in the back of her skull.

I arrived in the midst of the mess. Shower still running hot. Paramedics and police scrambling around in steam. Elizabeth sitting on the edge of the tub. Clutching Chester, our wily tom cat, to her chest. Crying, as Maggie was carried away.

Elizabeth puts her blond shock of curls against my chest, then looks up at me.

"But why does he kill the babies, Daddy?"

There are answers, but they don't come. I touch her hair. Kiss her forehead.

"Some things are a mystery," I say.

And we sleep.

✿

I wake an hour later to find that Elizabeth has moved on to other things. She is on the back deck. Sitting on the steps. Surrounded by paper and crayons. She is looking out over the pond. Drinking apple juice from her favorite cup. It is blue, shaped like the Cookie Monster, and so big that she has to hold it with both hands.

"Chester!" she calls between drinks, "Chester!"

Unlike Elizabeth and me, Chester has adjusted to the change quite nicely. The very first day we pulled into the driveway and Elizabeth opened the car door, Chester sprang out into the yard and started his run. We've been here a month and he hasn't stopped yet. We put out dishes of food and water, but he rarely touches them. These days, we only catch glimpses of him. A flash of gray darting through the grass. A shadow sneaking through the bushes. A tail twitching in the trees. Besides these fleeting moments, the only real signs we have that Chester is still around are the trophies he leaves behind.

At first it was feathers found under the deck. Then a field mouse left on the doorstep. But now, we have a body count that's rising. A robin, a dove. A ground squirrel, a mole. And now, it seems, Chester has found the bunny hole.

I drink a full cup of coffee while I stand there watching Elizabeth, and I survey the list in my head. *Refinish the deck. Mow the lawn. Plant the garden. Repaint the church. Shingle the steeple.* But today might be the day that Maggie wakes from her sleep. So Elizabeth and I will make the drive. To the hospital. We will sit in the room. Turn on the TV. And we will visit Maggie. For one hour. Until lunch, when Elizabeth and I will walk to

Jepetto's. She will order fried shrimp and mashed potatoes. I will pick at a salad. Force a burger down. And when the check comes, Elizabeth will insist that the waitress *box up the leftovers for Mom.*

We will take the leftovers to the hospital. Nurse Brooke and I will exchange kind smiles. She will take the leftovers from Elizabeth and promise to put them in the refrigerator for safekeeping.

Our visit will last well into the afternoon. There will be more TV. More talking. And finally, I will read a book out loud. To Elizabeth on my lap. And my wife asleep next to me. And for a short while, everything will feel right. The way it's supposed to be.

But all of this is yet to come. For now, I have a bunny to bury.

✧

I take the last shoe box from the closet. Put on my gloves and head for the door. I expect to see something gruesome. Like the other two. One found in the driveway, its head nearly torn from its body. The other on the back deck, missing its front legs and large patches of fur. But when I open the door, the bunny isn't on the step as Elizabeth has said. Instead, Chester has decided to be creative and he has left it next to the steps, under the rosebush. And unlike the others, this one looks all right. No blood. No missing limbs or missing fur. I hear Elizabeth padding around the corner of the house, so I scoop up the bunny and plop him into the box. His body makes a gurgling sound.

"Is it time for the funeral?" Elizabeth asks, as she runs up alongside me.

I snap on the lid and walk toward the church.

"Yes, it's time."

Elizabeth has only been to one real funeral. For her grandmother she barely knew. So she believes that every time something dies, we must have a funeral. We have only been in the country a short while, but already we've done this several times. Once for each of the bodies that Chester has left behind. And once for a dead deer we saw on the side of the road. All of the small animals are buried on the hill behind the pond. The deer, of course, was left to rot. *We don't have a big enough box for that,* Elizabeth said. *We'll just have to say some extra prayers.*

Our ramshackle church still has all the goods. The congregation split when the pastor married a woman downstate. The members moved on. Formed other churches. And everything was left behind. Pews. Bibles.

Candles. Robes. And hanging on the wall, against a velvety green curtain, is a big wooden cross. It is under this cross, on the altar, that Elizabeth and I place the shoe box.

Elizabeth kneels. Does the Sign of the Cross. I pick up the Bible we've used for funerals past. And then we make our way to the front pew. We sit side by side.

"What should we say this time?" I ask.

"I don't know," she says.

We sit for a moment in the warm light that slants through the tall stained glass windows. And we say nothing. Flies buzz near the ceiling. And I can hear something in the rafters. Mice, probably. And I wonder if I should leave the church door open for the night, so that Chester can do some more hunting.

Elizabeth takes the Bible and begins thumbing through the pages. She will find a passage. One that probably isn't even related to the task at hand. She will ask me to read it aloud, and that will be our prayer.

"Here, Daddy," Elizabeth says, as she hands me the book. "Read this one."

Her little finger points to one single line.

Behold, I shew you a mystery; We shall not all sleep, but we shall all be changed...

I read it. We let it sink in. Then I close the book, and I sit and stare at the cross. Imagine myself the head of this tiny congregation. Setting souls to rest. Bringing peace to tiny lives. And I think of how strange it is that we come to these places. Marriage. Children. Pews and hospital beds. Homes away from home. Our days in the city. The country.

Together or alone. And of how all of us in some way or another will find a dead bunny on our doorstep one day, and there is nothing we can do but pray, bury it, and move on.

"Some things *are* a mystery," Elizabeth says, as she reaches to hold my hand.

And from atop the altar, inside the shoe box, comes the most delicate scratching sound.

www.ingramcontent.com/pod-product-compliance
Lightning Source LLC
Chambersburg PA
CBHW052139170626
46812CB00004B/1507